TWISTED DELIGHTS: A THRILLING SHORT
STORY ANTHOLOGY
BY KIMBERLY BENNETT

Matthew,
Thank You for making my dream come true.
I love you

Twisted Delights: A Thrilling Short Story Anthology

CONTENTS

Twisted Delights: A Thrilling Short Story Anthology

AISLING

It had been a long and tiring trip across the Irish Sea. For the most part, we were always ready for anything on the *Evangeline*. A couple of men were on guard as night watchmen to signal the slumbering crew if danger should arise, but no one could have prepared us for what was to take place this fateful night.

The *Evangeline* had almost reached the shores of Ireland. We were excited by the anticipated landing. Suddenly, strange music, from what sounded like a French horn, moved like smoke upon the air currents and swept across the bridge, physically paralyzing the entire crew in its wake. The haunting melody made my stomach churn as I helplessly fell to the deck, like everyone else, with a loud thump. I ended up slumping in a sitting position with my back to the railing. I could see the entire deck. All my senses were intact, but my body was limp and useless. I was aware of my surroundings but could not interact with them because of the strange paralysis. This situation was quite unnerving, and I began to panic.

"It does no one any good to panic in a stressful situation," my father used to say. "Men can turn into sniveling children if given half a chance, so be a true man and be solid as a rock." My father's words renewed my original state of calm—and then I noticed that straight across the deck, a creature of some sort was climbing over the ship's railing like a spider spinning its web of deceit.

I sat in awe as the most stunningly beautiful woman slithered over the wooden railing. Her body was devoid of any clothing. Her skin was as pale as alabaster, and droplets of ocean water glittered in the moonlight, making her seem a translucent dream. My manhood told me she was not a dream, but I was powerless to do anything about it. Her feet touched the planks with a wet, sloppy noise, and she turned in a complete circle to survey the *Evangeline's* top deck. Her features were those of an angel, so delicate and fine. Her fiery red hair hung down her back in a sea of wild ringlets, almost reaching her waistline. Her buttocks glistened in the moonlight as she crouched down to investigate a member of the crew. I grew even more excited at the sight of her body creeping closer to me, man by man.

I forced my attention away from the creature and noticed that the *Evangeline* had begun to rock to and fro from the pounding of the waves, and a gentle rain started to fall down from the heavens, as if the sky had opened up to cry tears of sadness upon us. Nature knew what our destiny was, and so did I. I remembered ancient stories my grandfather told about a creature of the sea called a mermaid. Grandfather spoke of the mermaid in a way that had frightened me when I was younger. He explained that while these creatures were beautiful to look upon, their beauty masked an evil, black heart that did not contain a soul.

"They are damned to the smoking pits of hell," my grandfather roared. "They are agents of Satan, come to do his bidding by stealing the souls of young seamen. Be very careful, and keep a lookout for them when you ride the waves of life so that you may return home safe and make your mother happy."

A loud thunderclap woke me from my reverie. I scanned the deck for signs of the sea woman, but she must have slipped below deck. I heard her movements beneath me in the ship's hull. At any moment one of us could be released from our paralysis and send her to hell and rescue the others, but she didn't seem concerned with that. It bothered me that I couldn't see what instrument of death she wielded, but the noises from down inside the *Evangeline* told me that my friends were dying left and right.

I tried to shut out the cries of those who knew what was coming, but it was becoming impossible because the closer to the hull entrance she came, the louder the moans were. Even though silence came within a few minutes from each seaman, the haunting reality struck home like a spike being driven into my heart. The throbbing intensity of moments past came to a crashing halt when the unbearable situation stopped my thoughts. I turned my attention away from the noise of her ghastly work to wonder at the complexity of the situation.

I thought that all creatures of the earth came from God the father, and if that was so, what caused this one to be so hateful and violent? What caused her to climb aboard a ship's deck and take the life force from every seaman aboard who was being transported across the waters of God's own creation? Was she truly an angel from hell, or was she a troubled, misguided spirit who sought revenge against humans who were innocent of whatever tragedy that had claimed her as its victim? These questions may never be answered, but I asked them anyway.

A bolt of lightning streaked across the inky black sky and woke me from my thoughts. A little bit dazed from my intense ramblings, I noticed that the sea woman had begun her torment of those who were on deck. She must have dispatched all the souls from below because she crept about the top deck with a surety that was totally unnerving, and there was silence again from beneath the planks of the deck. Oblivious to the fact that dawn was upon us, she continued with her slaughter. I had heard the stories of sea creatures and the hellish torment they brought to humankind on the sea, but I never believed them until now.

Her next victim was my friend Genaro, who was closest to the hull's door on the right side. I tried to move, but I was still helpless. My manhood had shrunk back from the horror of the situation, and I was no longer aroused by the sea woman's beauty. I wanted to scream out to Genaro, but only silence came from my lips.

The sea woman hovered over Genaro and raised her arm. A flash of metal glinted in the moonlight as the mermaid brought her instrument of death down in a slashing motion. A slight noise came from my direction as the wind kicked up a bit and made a rope from one of the ship's sails slap into the mast. She turned, looked in my direction, surveyed her surroundings, and shrugged off the noise. I watched Genaro's eyes widen in fright as the sea woman disemboweled his helpless form in one swift and sure motion. The contents of his abdomen spilled forth onto the deck like homemade spaghetti from a cooking pot. The life in Genaro's eyes quickly disappeared as he realized what she had done. He sighed heavily, and he was gone. My heart skipped a beat at his untimely death, and sadness crept over my being.

Genaro was not the first to feel the sea woman's wrath. As grief hammered me, I looked away from his mutilated body and focused my eyes on the blood-soaked deck. The burgundy liquid saturated everything it came in contact with, and the plank boards looked as if they had been freshly painted with it. The ship had ceased its movement, causing a silence to sweep across what was left of the *Evangeline's* crew. My eyes moved to scan the deck. I trained my eye to see what had taken place to each and every seaman on deck. Many had their throats slit from ear to ear and some, like Genaro, had their abdomens cut, revealing their innards for the birds to prey upon. Speaking of birds, they had already begun to circle above the dead bodies, waiting for a chance to dive down and tear into flesh. Their eerie caws pierced the night sky as dawn crept upon us. A shimmer of gold on the horizon gradually grew with each moment that passed. The sea woman's work was almost completed. She had made her way around the railing and was coming to my position. As deadly as this woman was, I felt my desire grow again. The nearness of her body made me ashamed of my present state, but she was incredibly irresistible.

Maybe it was her beauty mixed with danger that caught me off guard, or maybe it was my age. I had just turned twenty-one last month and had already entered manhood like a stallion. Girls fawned over me at every port and tried their damnedest to claim me as their own. I longed for the freedom of the sea and struck out on my own. I claimed the sea as my wife at the tender age of sixteen. Five years I had spent with my beloved, and never once have I feared her like I did now.

The sea woman woke me from my ramblings by tripping over my long, lanky legs. She swore under her breath as she regained her composure. She stooped down to look at my face.

"You're a young one," the sea woman looked deeper into my eyes while brushing my hair away from my face. "and very handsome, as well. It's a pity your good looks are going to be wasted as feed for the birds."

Her demeanor was that of dominance. Never had I encountered a woman like her before; most were meek and giggly with innocence, but she was not meek or giggly; she was entirely enthralled with her accomplishments of the past night. She stood up and strutted by me as if I were the one on display, all the while keeping a keen eye on my form.

The sun was half raised now and streaked the sky with ribbons of gold, pink, and blue. The wind remained quiet for the time being, and the rocking of the boat was slight. The thunder had ceased its roaring long ago. As the sun rose higher, the deck became brighter with its crimson hue. The sea woman's body was covered in a pinkish wash of blood. Spatters of red clung to her delicate facial features, but as delicate as her features were, her heart was hard as a stone. She turned around and eyed her handiwork and, seeming quite pleased, returned to my helpless form. I still had no control over my limbs and could not defend myself against the sea woman's determination. She crouched down in front of me with one knee landing on the deck.

"I will explain myself only to you," she whispered to me, moving in close to my face. "You remind me of someone I once knew." The pain that shot through her face over that revelation was indescribable. Her hardness melted, and a more womanly attitude took her over. She seemed soft and gentle now. The closer to my face she came, the closer to release I came. Her hands grazed over my legs and up my abdomen. My control was usually limited, and I wasn't certain how long it would be before my body gave in to her caresses. Her hands landed on my chest, and she caressed a small patch of my hair that protruded from the V-neck of my shirt. She slid her hands down into my shirt and back up and out again. While I was physically unable to touch her, I was quiet certain I would unleash my manhood's desire if she continued with her caressing and probing. A sweet, impish smile took over her lips as she honed in on my state of arousal.

She slid her bent knee to lay her leg flat on the deck and sat next to me, impervious to the pool of blood that came from the seaman next to me. She was positioned with her left leg stretched out and resting against my right while facing me. From the corner of my eye I watched her feet as she wiggled her toes and flexed them forward and back. I moved my gaze slowly up her bloodstained, soft-skinned legs to her waist. The sea woman reached out her hand and wagged her finger at me as if I was being naughty.

The sun was fully risen now, and the sky was lit up by the radiant beams of a fresh morning. The sea woman's skin, that which hadn't been streaked with a pink hue from the evening's events, had turned from alabaster to a creamy ivory in the sunlight. Her translucence was replaced by a real solidness that wakened me from my thoughts of sexual desire. She still watched me intently, her impish smile spreading to reveal her pearl white teeth. It took my breath away.

"Do you want to know who I am and why I am here?" she asked. Inside I nodded yes to her question, but I still could not physically muster the motion. "Your people came to my homeland, raped our young women, tortured my mother in public, and decimated my tribe, all for greed and power." She shifted her position slightly from one hip to the other, seemingly uncomfortable with her posture.

"My mother, Queen Boudicca, struck back with a vengeance. She raised our people up and began to slaughter the intruders with my sister and me by her side." The anger in her voice was loud and clear, and she spoke as if she had been a queen herself.

"Before her death, she buried my sister's body and took me to the eastern edge of Ireland. Facing an inlet, she summoned her druid powers to change me into the creature that I am now. She instructed me to guard the waters of our home and dispatch all who would dare to come and strike tragedy on our people."

I watched as the sea woman's features had changed from softness to relentless anger and back to softness again. She had dropped her arms into her lap and stared down at her own nakedness.

"I am immortal and will forever swim this sea and protect my people at all costs." Her voice became less harsh. "You look at me as if I am a monster, but it is your people who are the monsters. I am only defending what I claim to be mine and what is dear to my heart." She raised her face up to look directly into my eyes. "I am not evil," she went on. "I have loved, I have laughed, and I have lived, but the time came for me to put away childish things and be strong."

Her gaze grew more intent as she peered into my own soul with her deep, moss green eyes. "I will spare your life and grant you your freedom, but if you ever dare to sail this way again, I will not be so gracious a second time."

An awkward silence fell between us, and she changed her demeanor as she continued to gaze intently into my eyes. She seemed more relaxed and sort of innocent. I truly felt sorry for her but still did not comprehend how she justified her actions. There was a deep sadness about her now as she changed her focus from me to the gathering flocks of scavengers, and she spoke once more.

"You remind of my betrothed. He was a fine, handsome Irish gentleman about your age. His face was masculine, like yours, but he carried the look of complete satisfaction with life." She sighed sadly.

"My name is Aisling, and I am a descendant of the Iceni tribe of Ireland. My betrothed and I were to marry the day after we were invaded." Her impish grin returned. "My sister and I had snuck out that fateful night for a bit of fun. Brighid was very mischievous and always in trouble with our mother.

"We climbed out our bedroom window and slipped into the night. I was to secretly meet my beloved by the water's edge. He had built a small campfire and was waiting for my sister and me."

I watched as the expression on her face continuously became softer and her posture increasingly relaxed. The desire that I had for her changed from intense hunger to a mere sliver of longing—despite her exotic beauty—with each word she spoke. She went on to reveal that while she was cavorting with her future husband by the water, her sister had vanished to meet her own beloved. She had failed to notice the massive ships that had crashed into her shores at twilight. Troops of invaders spilled forth from the bowels of the mighty sea transports; they forged on through the woods and into the villages to pillage, rape, and destroy all that they came in contact with.

By the time she had completed her story, her beloved was dead; she and her sister had been raped. Her mother, being publicly humiliated, was bent on death and destruction of her own making. Aisling seemed mentally and emotionally exhausted. She rose from her spot, walked to the railing, and leaned over the edge.

"I have never spoken to anyone about this before. I have never explained myself to anyone. Never forget me, and always remember the danger that lurks in the waters of Ireland for those who want to dominate her and her people." And with that, she leapt up on the railing, stretched out her arms, and floated into the air like a graceful swan. I heard her splash into the sea, and she was gone, releasing me from my paralytic state. The thought of my homeland never sounded so good.

NIGHTMARE

I am walking barefoot in a knee-length nightgown of lavender satin. The cloth of my nightgown brushes my skin with each steady step I take and sends shivers of delight up my spine. The fabric feels cool and silky to the touch.

The ground has a chill to it, and there are many twigs, pinecones, and needles scattered about. I tread over them as if I were gliding on air. I do not wince or hesitate because I feel no pain. The strong odor of pine permeates the air and invades my nostrils with its familiar scent. A thick fog descends upon the ground and swirls about my body, wrapping me in its suffocating embrace while creating a curtain in which I can only see a few feet in front of me. My heart is racing, and I can feel my breath heavy in my chest. The atmosphere is silent, dead silent, except for my footsteps on the earth.

I am traveling on a pathway leading into a wooded area. My destination is unknown, and uneasiness creeps in on my self-consciousness as my heart rate increases. A slight breeze sweeps in and sends chills up and down my body. My nightgown gives me little protection as goose bumps rise and fall on my skin.

My breasts harden, and my nipples form tiny buttons that poke through the front of my gown.

Confusion peaks within me like the surge of a tide coming into shore. Anticipation of what will happen next invades my mind. I feel like a zombie walking in a world of desolation. I feel like a robot unable to control my own will or thought processes.

The fog begins to clear a little, and up ahead I can make out the faint outline of a small, dilapidated home. I have seen it before. Familiarity rushes in, and my heart ceases it's hard drumming in my chest. It slows to a steady rate, and my heavy breathing subsides.

The sight of the abandoned home comes into full view as I step through a veil of fog and into a clearing. The home is well weathered from lack of care. Paint has long been chipped off by the elements, leaving the outside stripped of its beauty. Its owners have left it to rot in solitude. The lap siding is missing here and there, and in between the slats I can see an amber glow. The roof is collapsed on one side, exposing the home's innards to weather. From inside the shack I can hear a child whimpering, and a shuffling of feet reaches my ears. I hesitate at the door, but reach out for the rusty knob anyway. I grasp the knob and turn it. The knob turns hard, not wanting to open up and let me in. The door creaks and groans in protest as I give it a hard shove, and the bottom of the door scrapes on the wooden floor like nails going down a blackboard.

I am hit with the fragrance of dust, age, and rodent excrement. Fear creeps into my being but I am unable to stop my movements. I can't turn and run, for I have no control over my body. I am compelled by an unknown force to enter. My heart rate rapidly increases again as my fight-or-flight instinct kicks in.

I step through the doorway and time seems to stand still. Rat carcasses litter the floor. Ten feet in front of me is a child who appears to be dirty and bruised. The child is a girl about seven years of age, and her waist-length hair hangs about her form in disarray. Tears stream down her filthy cheeks, and she lets out another whimper. Her clothing is partially torn from her body, exposing her bare skin. Behind her is a faceless man with his arms about the girl's shoulders. He is dressed in black from head to toe. He wears an overcoat that drapes about his form as if he were contained inside a shroud. He has placed her facing away from him as he slides a razor-sharp knife gently across her bare neck. In the wake of the weapon a pink welt line appears, but no blood is spilled.

Fear is thick in the air and emanates from the young girl and myself. I want to help her but I am unable to do so. I am powerless at the sight and begin to cry tears of shame.

In the distance I can hear a banging sound. Bang … bang … bang! The sound steadily grows into a volume of annoying proportions. The sound pierces my mind like a hammer driving in a nail, and I blink my eyes open as reality rushes in. I feel a jolt of relief wash over me as I sit upright in my bed. I am home. The nightmare always comes and goes like that. I hate it with a passion.

A faint uneasiness remains with me as I rise and dress for the day. I scuttle about my bedroom trying to forage for warm clothing. Bang … bang … bang! I know, even before I poke my head out the window, that there is snow on the ground and that the shutters in the living room are pounding out their frustration against my grandmother's old home. I pull on my well-worn, tattered jeans and a warm sweater that lie on my dresser top and, while slipping into my socks and boots, I can't help but stop and shudder at the thought of the poor little girl I was unable to save.

Sometimes my nightmare is so real I can still smell the smells of that old, dilapidated home and can still feel the chill of the air and the dampness of the fog. The girl's whimpers will most definitely remain with me for the rest of the day. I can only hope and pray that the next time I sleep it will be peaceful, but my hopes and prayers usually are useless. I am a captive to my subconscious and a prisoner to the evil being in my nightmare.

My thoughts continually focus back on my nightmare as I make my way down the wooden staircase and into the living room. Everything that happens within my nightmare remains the same except for the children. Sometimes it's a boy and sometimes it's a girl. There is something different about this last one. It somehow seemed more real. I can't shake from my mind the little girl's whimpering and the look of fear in her eyes. I pull back the heavy drapes that keep the warm in and the drafts down and open the window. The breeze that enters is an unwelcome visitor as it sends chills up my arms and across the room. I quickly pull the shutters closed, latch them securely, and close the window.

I walk toward the fireplace and mutter a curse. I pick up the poker next to the ash pail and poke and prod until I find some orange embers remaining in the fireplace. I put the poker back and retrieve four large logs from a stack of wood next to the fireplace. I toss them in and return to my thoughts about the villainous being in my nightmare. Although I have never seen his face, the mysterious man in my nightmare seemed more ominous in the darkness of the room. I felt like he was peering into my soul as I stood in that shack as a helpless voyeur while waiting for the obvious to take place.

I shift my attention to the growing fire and attend to it with care, poking at it with the poker and sweeping ash that has strayed too far from its home. The chill has died down some as time marches on, and the small fire turns into a roaring and crackling beast, biting and licking anything that comes into its domain. I reach for the teapot resting on the mantle. "Empty," I groan in protest. I shuffle toward the kitchenette and turn the faucet on. The pipes in the home began to rumble and hiss like a jungle predator, but their moaning settles down and becomes gently flowing water. I fill the teapot and return to the fireplace and hang it in its spot.

I work my way around the living room, tidying up a bit while waiting for my water to boil, shaking dust from the sofa coverlet and sweeping yesterday's dust from the floor. It takes about fifteen minutes, and by then my water is ready, whistling like a crazed banshee until I retrieve it from its hook. I pour my water into my teacup and add two teaspoons of honey and a squirt of lemon. While dipping my tea bag in and out of the steaming cup, I sink down into my grandmother's old recliner and let its healing comfort save me from my own psyche.

My self-imposed exile to my dearly departed grandmother's home is not only to heal and save myself, but to save my well-to-do family from societal ruin because they have a crazy in their midst. No one calls me anymore, and my father's visits have dwindled down to two times per month. My younger sister has shut me out of her life, ashamed that she too may come under the spell of the nightmare. My grandmother was the only one who understood, because she had the same nightmare. She described it as a psychic blessing, one that could be used for good, but all it did for her was cause her to grow slowly insane and pass away with no one but me to care for her belongings.

I take a sip of my tea and sink deeper into the recliner while pulling the afghan off the back of the chair and covering myself up to my chest. I know it's strange, but that chair has always made me feel cared for, comforted, and understood since my grandmother's death three years ago. Maybe some of her psychic energy remains in her home, dwelling in her old belongings and reaching out in understanding toward anyone who would dare take up residency.

My eyelids begin to droop, and I set my cup on the end table as I drift off to sleep again. The warmth of the fire, the comfortable old chair, and tea and an afghan make for a good slumber, but not if your dream world is etched with insidious evil. I am paralyzed from head to toe, and my body feels as if heavy weights hang off of all my limbs, and yet I feel as if I am floating, light as a feather on air. My destination is well known, and I shiver at the thought. Will this time be my turn? Not being able to break free of my own fears to save a child, will I then be condemned to the same fate? I am powerless as my consciousness overtakes me, and I do not find myself in the fog or in my nightgown, but fully dressed and bound to a rickety kitchen chair in that godforsaken hellhole of a shack.

The same odors and atmosphere remain, and my heart pounds against my chest in desperation. I look around frantically for my captor. Maybe by seeing him it would muster courage and power, enough for me to make an escape, but he is nowhere to be seen.

As far as I can make out, it seems to be mid-afternoon. The sun hangs high in the sky above the collapsed roof. My wrists are bound behind me with some type of hemp rope, and my ankles and torso are bound to the chair by electrical tape. I squirm and wriggle as if I am a fish out of water, but to no avail. It is useless. I cannot escape the chair, so I wait for my captor to make his ominous appearance.

As time passes, my anxiety grows to monstrous proportions and my irritation at being kept bound like a felon mounts. I can hear noises outside, and the fear inside me rises. I am now sweating profusely while the fire I am sitting near sputters and crackles and dominates the room with its energy. To the right of me is the fireplace and to the left is an open space. In front of me is the main entrance, and I'm not quite sure what is behind me because I cannot turn my head around far enough to discern anything.

I feel a hand snake its fingers into the hair at the back of my neck and make their way up to my occipital bone. As I hear crackling of vertebrae, a hard yank brings my head upward and back toward the faceless being. His breath caresses my cheek with the strong presence of alcohol, like a drunkard who has spent a week's wages on the poison of his choice. All I can see is a satanic sneer out of my left eye that could bring the most saintly of saints to his knees.

My captor says nothing, nothing at all, which adds to my mounting anxiety and frustration. While I feel utterly helpless, I can move my body parts at will, which means there could be some hope for me if I could just break free of the binding on my limbs. The hold on my hair is released, and I shake my head. The evil form moves from behind my chair with his back toward me. He picks up the poker leaning against the left side of the fireplace, and after successfully prodding the embers and the remaining wood in the fire; he replaces the poker and turns his attention toward me.

Walking slowly around my chair, like a military officer on patrol, he seems to be inspecting every inch of my body. He stops to my right, and I feel a sickening sensation rise in my belly. He leans in, and I can still only make out his cruel and devilish mouth that leers at me like a lion waiting to devour its prey.

"I have been waiting for you." His voice is raspy and full of intent. I say nothing as I wait for the inevitable.

Relief washes over me as he walks back around me. This time he stops at my left and, surprisingly, turns and stomps off in the direction of the back of the house. While he marches away from me like a general gone mad, I take the chance that he is out of sight and sound and use my body to scoot the chair closer to the fireplace. With my back now near the opening of the fireplace, I try to force my hands as close to the fire as possible. I feel that risking a few burns for the hope that I can free myself far outweighs the cost of doing nothing. So, as hot as it gets, I move my arms closer to the fire. Within seconds I can smell burning flesh and hemp, while the ropes on my wrists release their viselike hold. I shake my arms free of their bonds and pat out the small flames with my hands. I can feel no pain at this point but can see that it will soon set in because blisters have already begun to form on my hands and arms. I quickly make use of my newfound freedom and reach down to free my torso and ankles. Ripping tape off like a crazed animal, I work fast and am soon on my feet and looking for a weapon.

The house is empty except for some chairs and a few broken pieces of furniture. I choose a nice-sized wooden leg of some sort and swish it around the air like a knight of the round table. I guess those self-defense classes I took a few years back will come in handy at this point in time. I ignore the burning and painful blisters as I wait for the entity of evil to return. I have a surprise for him that he will hopefully not enjoy. I look for a good place to perch myself for the time being and find a suitable spot on the other side of the fireplace.

I am startled back to reality when I feel the ominous presence of evil enter the room. I peer around the corner of the fireplace and hug its back side with my body. As I peek ever so slightly around the corner, I see the man moving through the room, coming in my direction as he begins his tirade. He tosses chairs and pieces of broken furniture this way and that. I jump each time one clatters to the floor or hits a wall. My superhuman nerve is failing me, so it's now or never. I swivel around and move toward the other side of the fireplace carefully, tiptoeing like a little church mouse until I am positioned on the opposite side of where I was originally. I poke my head out and hold my breath at the same time. His back is toward me and I rush out, swinging my weapon like a madwoman. I come down hard on his form with a few good blows, and he crumples to the floor like a sack of potatoes. I go to swing a few more times, and he hops into the air like a jackrabbit. Regaining his composure as he lands on his feet, he reaches out and backhands me to the floor with a loud clap. My body tumbles like a rag doll across the floor, and I lose my grip on the wooden leg. I scramble to get up, but the evil one looms above my body like the grim reaper.

"I have to admit you have spunk," he spits out in my direction. "You are far more of a challenge then all the little ones I so enjoy entertaining." With that last remark he throws his head back in a satanic laugh and takes a posture of power over me. I don't fall for it. As scared as I am, I will win this fight—if not for me, then for all the innocents before me who had to endure their pain in this miserable place. It has to end now.

As I lie in a heap of pain on the floor, I muster the energy to pick up an old, rusted butcher knife I happened to fall upon. Reaching under my backside, I slide the knife out carefully and, with a force unbeknownst to me, plunge the weapon directly into his heart. A scream peals out from his lips like a person being skinned alive as he stumbles backward, away from my helpless form. I am physically and emotionally drained, but it is not over yet. While his body drops to the floor in agony and blood spills from his wound, I rise unsteadily to my feet. I place a few good, hard kicks into his ribs as he squirms in pain. I let loose on him with the fury of a volcanic eruption as my body and mind slip into a slow-motion movie.

Grabbing his hair with both my hands, I drag his helpless, squirming form over to the front of the fireplace. His screams of agony rise to deafening proportions, and I ignore his cries for help. I let my grip go and give him a few more hard kicks to the ribs. He peals out a few more squeals of sheer pain before rising to his feet and removing the knife from its home in what seems to be one swift motion. Stunned, I take a few steps back to let reality sink in, and then I charge him while grabbing the chair that I was bound to earlier. I scoop up the chair, and in one forceful motion I slam the rickety piece of furniture into his side so hard that he rocks straight into the fireplace. Pieces of wood splinter in all directions, and I shield my eyes from their flight with my hands.

Racked with pain and the certainty that his unending rampage of torture is about to end, he collapses with a thud on the hearth and lets out a gasp. I can't believe my eyes. It is finally over. The evil man in the cloak will never return to hurt or kill another innocent ever again.

Not sure of what to do now or how to return to the safety of my grandmother's home, I turn and begin to walk away. A faint rumbling rises underneath the floorboards, and the planks begin to bulge and snap from their places. I run, with a limp no less, to the front door, and an explosion lets loose and propels my body through the air like a dart. I tumble to the ground as the house behind me goes up in flames.

My fear and anxiety release their confining grip on my very soul while relief and warmth rush in to soothe my wounds. I open my eyes and find myself on the floor of my grandmother's living room. The fire has died out, and a chill sits in the room like a heavy weight. All I can do is sob with the satisfaction that now I can live my life, and live it to the fullest, without looking back at the horror of my nightmare, because it will never come again. No more innocent children will be tortured or die because the evil man is dead himself. His soul has gone back to its home in hell, never to return again. I am now free of my nightmare and can move on in peace.

I rise from the floor in great physical pain and manage to gingerly sink down into my grandmother's old recliner. I let its healing powers take care of my emotional wounds with comfort, warmth, and love. I am free at last.

THE MEDUSA VIRUS

Beautiful crystalline snowflakes had begun to fall, and the mountain air was a chilly thirty degrees Fahrenheit. The winter semester was finally over. I had made many new friends at St. Brennan's College for Young Women. The one I was closest with was my roommate, Ilyana.

St. Brennan's was a prestigious college filled with historic architecture, antiquities, and exquisite fine art from the Early English period dated 1200–1275 AD. The building featured lancet windows with colorful stained glass supported by elaborate stonework. The four corners of the building seemed to be held up by slender towers topped with spires that added to its Gothic allure. From the walls in the main building hung many fine art reproductions and tapestries that kept down drafts of chilly air.

The courtyard, which was surrounded by a periodic Gothic colonnade, was our favorite place to study. The tranquility that exuded from the indigenous plants and trees, as well as the gently flowing water fountain, was enough to relax and make one become almost entranced. The courtyard had many seating arrangements among the foliage and shrubbery, and the wooden walkways were lined with pink, purple, and blue flowers.

The dormitory where Ilyana and I shared a room was built in the late 1400s and had a Tudor feel to it. The entrances to the dormitory grounds were gained by passing through a medieval gatehouse and continuing into a small courtyard and up the steps. The estate was bursting with English countryside heritage, and I was enthralled with the magical atmosphere every time I set foot inside the gatehouse. It was as if I were in a fantasyland dream every day I spent at St. Brennan's.

I spied Ilyana in a hallway near our lunchroom in the main building. As I walked down the hall toward my friend, I passed three large lancet windows with the noon sun streaming in. The sun's rays exploded into the corridor like a spectacular fireworks display. I was in awe at the beauty of it all.

"Hey, girlfriend!" I said to Ilyana. Her fair hair and delicate features always made me jealous. I was pretty enough, I suppose. I didn't have trouble finding dates, but Ilyana was always a favorite with the boys. The male gender preferred blondes to redheads in the English countryside.

"Hey, Grace!" Ilyana exclaimed. She turned to me with one of her gracious grins and patted my shoulder. "What's up?" she asked.

Ilyana's blonde hair was tied loosely at her nape in a fluffy ponytail that swished this way and that when she turned her head. She was warmly dressed in a turquoise cable-knit sweater that matched her eyes. Her jeans flared at the bottom, and beneath them she always wore black Italian leather boots indoors. She was sure to change out of the expensive footwear and pull on wool-lined boots for outside, as we all did.

I mimicked her attire, but not in color. My sweater was a brilliant hue of moss green, which smartly complimented my doe-like brown eyes and medium copper-colored, shoulder-length hair. I wore flared jeans as well, but preferred to adorn my feet with Reebok cross-trainers for comfort.

Ilyana said good afternoon to our classmates, and we turned to make the long trek to the library at the other end of the main building. We needed to stop and check our grades before making the last arrangements for our winter vacation. The final grades were always posted in a book held in the head librarian's charge for privacy and were only to be viewed by the owner.

For winter, Ilyana and I always chose to stay at St. Brennan's for vacation. Both our families were jet-setters year round and were not available for our homecomings until the summer. This year was different. Ilyana and I were going to take a little trip into a small village that was tucked at the bottom of St. Brennan's mountain.

We laughed and talked about what was in store for us over the next four weeks as we made our way to the library. When we arrived, it was as if the library doorway was an entrance to another world, or perhaps another time period. The doorway consisted of a double pointed arch, which spread open into a great expanse of bookcases and antique furniture. Tables and chairs were grouped together in little patches among large bookcases that housed massive volumes of ancient and modern works.

To the right of the great doorway was the head librarian's desk. "Good afternoon, Mrs. Collins," I said. Mrs. Collins was a short and stout woman of fifty years. She always had a warm presence about her and welcomed us every time we graced her domain.

"Good afternoon, girls," Mrs. Collins replied. "And what might two beautiful young things be up to this fine afternoon?"

Ilyana and I grinned at Mrs. Collins. "Oh, just checking in on our performance for this past semester," Ilyana replied, giving the older woman a wink.

"You two are silly." Mrs. Collins shuffled pages in the final grade book and stopped to peer at one page in particular. "You both are the best students of the entire campus, and I don't know why you waste your time checking grades when you could be chasing boys!"

And with that, we giggled a Wilma-and-Betty giggle and waited. Mrs. Collins gave us both our final grades for the semester, and when she saw that we were satisfied, she said farewell and withdrew herself from her desk to attend to business in her office.

Ilyana and I were both pleased with our grades. In fact, we were pleased with our grades most of the time. We both were perfectionists and made sure our GPA never dropped below 3.8. Perfectionism is one of our similar traits and what originally made our friendship begin to blossom.

Even though Ilyana and I were great friends, our friendship had a dark side to it. At certain times Ilyana became reclusive and withdrawn, almost as if she was in great emotional torment. When I had originally asked about her foul mood, she would shrug it off and ask to be left alone. During those times, Ilyana read from an old book she claimed was passed down generation to generation by the women in her family. She forbade me to touch it, much less look at it from across the room. I agreed to her demand. After all, if she wanted to be private on that front, it was fine by me. The book looked too creepy anyway, but my curiosity sometimes became almost unbearable.

The current afternoon was the first occasion of my almost unbearable curiosity. After Ilyana and I retrieved our final grades from Mrs. Collins, we retired to our dorm room to discuss our winter plans.

"I can talk to you later about winter holiday," Ilyana said to me as she crawled into her bed. "I have a monstrous headache and need to get a few winks." And with that, she passed out into a deep sleep.

I waited until she snored lightly and crept to her closet door. I fished around underneath the carpeting for her trunk key. Claiming my prize, I inserted the key into the lock and opened the trunk.

Ilyana had many wondrous treasures in her trunk, some of which she had shared. But there were some strange items she did not. I pulled out an antique talisman from under some fabric. I wasn't quite sure if it warded off evil or made the possessor powerful. I put it back. My hands passed over a rather large and pointy artifact. I pulled it out. It was a sword; a rather long and very sharp handcrafted sword. The sword was a magnificent piece of work, with a handle made of what appeared to be bone. Questions came to my mind, but it wasn't what I was after. I put it back. I would find out about those two items later.

I was after her book. I knew it was wrong to rummage through her stuff, but I had never hidden anything from Ilyana and felt cheated that she did not find me trustworthy enough to divulge her deepest, darkest secrets to me. Nothing in her past or present would make me love her any less. We were like sisters.

On her bed, Ilyana tossed toward the wall, and her movements made me pause. A few moments passed, and I resumed my work. As I dug deeper, my hands reached the bottom of her trunk and found no book. I decided to tap lightly on the bottom of the trunk for a hidden compartment. Something that secretive must surely be hidden well. As I tapped, I struck gold! There was a secret compartment. I found a corner and pulled the top off. There it was! The very book!

A nagging feeling of betrayal squelched my excitement. I would never betray Ilyana. I still couldn't get over the fact that she wouldn't share this book with me. I would never tell anyone about the book, or even about what was in it. So why would Ilyana be distrustful?

I pushed aside my guilt and pulled out the book. Huddled in the corner of my friend's closet and hunched over her prized possession, I opened it.

The cover had no lettering whatsoever on the outside. It must have been read a gazillion times over, because it was well worn from age and use. The book was large and smelled musty, as if it had been stored in a moldy basement for years on end. As I thumbed through it quickly, I noticed the pages were an icky yellow shade and were in delicate condition. I was very careful not to tear or bend the pages.

I turned back to the very first page and was greeted by a rather enormous family tree that took up approximately the first three pages and consisted of females only. It dated back to the thirteenth century and seemed to keep track of an inherited illness. Was Ilyana sick? Did she not want to worry me with her illness? Is that why she never shared this book with me?

Guilty thoughts made their way into the forefront of my mind again, but I quickly shoved them back. If Ilyana was sick, then I would do whatever I could to help her. So I read on.

I discovered that a virus had been present in the blood of the females in Ilyana's family line since the nineteenth century. The virus stemmed from a curse put upon Ilyana's great-great-great-great-grandmother by a witch who had been sentenced to burn at the stake. Ilyana's ancestor had played a significant role in the execution and was punished by the sorceress for eternity.

I sat cross-legged and in shock on the closet floor. My thoughts returned to Ilyana and her health. Would she be OK? Could modern medicine cure her if she was ill? Surely a curse from a witch could not carry itself to the modern day? Could it?

I peeked around the corner of the closet, and my gaze rested on the sleeping Ilyana. She was so beautiful and never showed any signs of illness. What if it was terminal? A wave of panic gripped my very being, and I squeezed my eyes shut to cut a tear off from sliding down my cheek. I rubbed my eyes and shut the book.

I had done enough for one day. Ilyana would awaken any minute now. I would keep my venture to myself. Stuffing Ilyana's articles carefully back where they had rested before, I closed her trunk. I stood up and closed the closet and returned her key. I opened our dorm door and stepped out into the hall.

I walked through the darkened hallway and made my way down the large staircase and into the kitchen. It was empty. It had been dark outside for about a half an hour and I knew no one else was there. Everyone had already packed and left for the holiday retreat to their respective homes.

I busied myself with making a snack and grabbing a soda. I could hear the television on in the great room. I knew without looking that our head mistress, Miss Kensington, would be fast asleep in her recliner. Actually, she wasn't fast asleep. She was drunk and passed out to the world. Her hangover would guarantee her foul mood in the morning.

I finished up in the kitchen and walked into the great room and watched some TV. I snickered when Miss K started to snore. She always sounded like Fred Flintstone, and I waited for tapestries to come flying across the room.

I was only lying on the couch for a few moments when my eyes became heavy. When I woke hours later, my eyes flickered open and I focused on the grandfather clock in a corner past the television. Someone had turned it off. Who? It was just past midnight, and Miss K was still in her recliner. The moon's silver light streamed in the French doors and spread across the carpeting like a fungus.

I heard a rustling noise outside the French doors that opened from the great room onto a patio and into a small courtyard. What was that? I asked myself. Still not quite awake, I unsteadily stood from the couch and walked to the French doors. When I peered out, I saw the most hideous sight anyone could ever see! I gasped in horror and clasped my hands over my mouth. I stumbled back from the doors and ran into the couch. Falling onto the couch in a sitting position, I forced myself to stand again, almost immediately.

As I stood, I was frozen in terror. Outside the French doors walked a hideous creature. What it was, I didn't know.

I didn't want to wake Miss K up. She would never understand. She would probably laugh at me and go to her room to continue her sleep-off. I overcame my frozen state and crept over to her recliner and reached out to touch her arm. What I touched wasn't skin. It felt like rough stone. What had happened to Miss K? I shrugged my shoulders in exasperation and decided that I would go investigate the creature's whereabouts.

I was fully awake within the few minutes it took me to get on my parka, boots, mittens, and hat. Actually, my adrenaline was sky-high, and I was buzzing with energy. I opened the front door and in came a gust of wind, sending snowflakes into the foyer. I quickly stepped outside and closed the door. I walked around the house on the stone walkway that led to the patio. My footsteps crunched in the snow as I made my way to the patio and into the courtyard.

When I came to the courtyard I noticed that the creature left no footprints, but slithering tracks that fish tailed this way and that. Fear struck me like a cannonball, but it was too late to turn back.

I followed the tracks through the gatehouse and into a tree line edged by silver birch and field maple that then led into a forest of Scots pine. The air held a chill that was indescribable, and the wind was numbing. I forged on.

The tracks seem to make their way to a site of ancient ruins, about a mile from the estate but still on college grounds. The ruins were hidden in between some rocky outcroppings surrounded by dense Scots pine. It was a favorite place for students to make out.

Some male students had brought Ilyana and me to that very site for some after-school activities, but we would only let them get so far and say so long. We would flee into the safety of the woods with waves of regret and the sounds of girlish laughter.

A noise inside the ruins ahead brought my attention back to the present. I could see a form just beyond what was left of a stone wall. The creature was nearly seven feet tall. Its head had no hair, but in its place were several snakes hissing and snapping at one another. The body was snakelike and the color of sea foam green. On its back was a sheathed sword that was very similar to the one I'd found in Ilyana's trunk.

The moonlight sent silver shafts of light through the pine trees and into the ruins, making faint pools of platinum on the uneven terrain. I reached the outer stone wall and pressed my body against its cold, hard, jagged surface. I peered into the ruins through a gap in the wall.

I heard the creature start to weep. Could that be? That awful creature was sad? That horrible creature, which could probably kill a person with just a look, was crying? The creature turned in my direction and paused its onslaught of tears.

I shrank back from the opening and hugged tighter to the wall. The jagged stone made tiny tears into my parka. Did it know I was there? More questions flooded my mind, but I was too petrified to answer myself. I couldn't think at the present. I was just plain scared stiff.

"Grace?" the creature called out to me in a raspy voice. The voice was familiar. "Grace, are you there?" I heard some rustling and twigs snapping. "Grace, don't be afraid."

I knew that voice. Could it be? No, I could not imagine that voice or that creature attached to my beautiful friend in any way. I peered into the gaping hole again, and as the creature slithered into a pool of moonlight I saw that the facial features were a distortion of Ilyana's.

No! I cried to myself. Tears streamed down my face like droplets of hot water. My face flushed with fear, anger, and other emotions. My arms and legs were rubbery, and I couldn't move. I was mesmerized by the creature's fluidity of movement.

It spoke again. "Grace, don't look into my eyes or come too close."

I felt like I was in a slow-moving cinematic climax. The kind sinister dreams are made of. Nightmares where you can't move, you can't breathe, and you most certainly can't speak.

It came closer. "Grace, I know it's you." The raspy voice was full of shame and sorrow.

"Ilyana?" I finally managed to squeak out. "What … What are you?"

"Grace, I can explain," Ilyana said. "You will find all you need to know in my book. The one   I made you promise never to touch." Ilyana's figure stopped its movement and paused with its arms outstretched, as if pleading for sympathy.

"Ilyana?" A full flood of tears came. I wiped furiously at my face, soaking up tears with my gloved hands.

"Grace, don't cry." The creature seemed pained but refused to move any closer in my direction. "You must do something for me."

I stood beyond the other side of the stone wall, listening to the creature's voice, uncertain that it was really Ilyana. My mind said it wasn't, but my heart said it was my best friend. My soul ached with confusion and pain.

I gathered some courage, straightened, and stepped through the gap in the wall. I made it a point to not look directly into the creature's eyes, as instructed, even though my morbid curiosity was in full blossom. I held it in check.

The creature stood in front of me and made one quick movement to remove the sword from its home. Metal scraped like nails going down a blackboard. I assumed the sheath was made from some type of coarse material because of the sound it made.

"Grace, you have to do me favor." The creature swayed in my direction. I took a step back and touched the wall with my back. Up against a wall and nowhere to hide or run. Frantic thoughts of impending doom raged through my mind like a train.

"Stop right there!" I managed to squeak out, rather loudly. The creature stopped its movements and swayed in a stationary spot within a few feet of me. My head was slightly lowered, but I still could see the creature's shape with my peripheral vision. It stretched out an arm, pointing the sword toward me.

"You must behead me," the creature cried out. Its words were a pitiful mixture of anguish and harshness. She wasn't asking; she was commanding me to take her head off.

"Are you insane?" I asked it. "If you are Ilyana, and grant you your facial features are quite similar, I would never do something so terrible to my friend—or anyone else, for that matter." I heard a gasp from the creature and an onslaught of unrecognizable moaning flowed from its lips.

Pity and sadness gripped my soul. This thing was definitely in some type of emotional or mental pain. What if it was Ilyana? My heart went out to it. I reached out and grabbed the sword handle.

"Before I do this ..." I paused. "I want some answers. Why? How? And did you turn Miss K into stone?" My voice quivered at the last question, because at this point I knew in my heart that she had done the deed.

"I am cursed and will be until my death. I will continually turn into this hideous creature before you every time there is a full moon." Ilyana took a slow, deep breath. The hissing of the snakes intensified, almost as if they didn't want me to hear Ilyana's words.

"I will hunt and turn anyone that comes across my path into stone." Ilyana's head dropped as if she was ashamed. "I hate my curse. I hate the death and sorrow I cause, and I can't bear it anymore." Her words tugged at my spirit and made my heart break at their speaking. Ilyana reached out to touch me, but recoiled immediately. She went on to explain that her touch was just as deadly as a look from her evil eyes and that she had been waiting for someone to come along to free her from her state.

Her freedom could only be gained by her death. The sword she stowed in her trunk, that I currently held, was the only instrument capable of the job. I paused to think of my friend. I cried tears of rage and sadness as I raised the sword and beheaded Ilyana. One of the snakes struck my arm and bit through my parka as the sword sliced through the air. I dropped the sword and grabbed my arm to stop the flow of blood.

"Sorry," escaped my lips as Ilyana's head dropped to the ground and rolled to my feet. Her body slumped to the ground and transformed in front of me, twisting and twitching like it was convulsing. The creature's body metamorphosed into the human form of Ilyana.

The snakelike extensions of her head returned to their natural state of blonde hair. Her skin faded from sea foam green to pale cream. Yes, it was Ilyana. I bent over Ilyana's lifeless body and head and reached out to touch her beautiful face. Stroking her cheek, a wave of emotion gripped my being. I could not control myself any longer. Tears came in buckets and anger raged through me. Why did Ilyana have to die?

I left her remains where they lay and gathered an enormous pile of rocks to cover her body. The ground was frozen and almost impossible to dig through. It took me about an hour, but I managed to cover Ilyana's entire body. Hopefully, no one would disturb the pile for a long time to come.

I made the long walk back to the dorm, dragging the sword behind me. The wind ripped through the air with a loud whistle and blew about me like a tornado. When I entered the front door, I shucked my winter wear in the foyer. The dorm was still silent. I went to my room and cleaned Ilyana's sword.

Sadness racked my body as I retrieved the trunk from the closet and replaced the sword. I fumbled for the false bottom and pulled out the book. My arm was throbbing. I rose and tossed the book on my mattress and pulled up my sleeve.

The flow of blood had subsided, but the swollen puncture marks remained. The snake's venom coursed through my body like a raging storm. I could feel the vile liquid tunneling through my veins. I dropped to my bed and lay down to rest and think. I had run out of tears to cry and decided to read some more of Ilyana's book.

Sliding my hand over the top of my comforter, I found and stroked the book's cover. I dragged the book my way and turned on my side to light my lamp.

I made a horrifying discovery halfway through my reading as the sun began to rise.

The curse was virus-like. There was no cure, no antibiotic that could flood my body and destroy the evil, no surgery or any type of treatment that could stop it. The curse would not end with my friend's death.

THE DEVIL'S INVITATION

Ding-dong! The familiar ring of the doorbell reverberated off the walls on the main floor of my ranch-style home. I stood in the kitchen with the last of the trick-or-treat candy in a bowl in hand. I walked into the living room and opened the front door.

"Trick or treat!" bellowed the youngsters. There were three children dressed in fantasy costumes. The first child was a little girl dressed as a Disney princess. She was beautiful with her blue bodice, yellow flowing skirt, and black wig with a red bow.

"My, what do we have here?" I smiled at the princess. "Little Miss Snow White has come to my house, and I am not fit to hostess royalty." I bowed from the waist, and the little girl giggled as I stood upright and put a large candy bar in her pumpkin bucket. Snow White moved to the side so her comrades could receive their treats.

"What a cute little pixie!" I spoke to the smallest of the three as she stepped forward with a shy grin. She was wearing a short green dress cut off at the knees and butterfly wings. I dropped another large candy bar into a pumpkin bucket and acknowledged the next character.

"A handsome young knight you are!" The impish boy blushed and turned away from me. "Good sir, would you like a candy bar?" I called after him as he began to walk away.

"Don't worry about him," said Snow White. "He's really shy, and he thinks you're pretty." The other children giggled. "If you give me the candy bar, I'll give it to him later, OK?" I nodded in agreement and handed Snow White the candy bar.

As soon as the two girls received their candy, they turned and ran screaming for the next house. They met up with the knight at the sidewalk, and I watched them as they laughed and squealed with delight and forged on in their quest for some more Halloween treats. I noticed that Snow White made good on her promise and gave the knight his candy before they made it to my next-door neighbor's house.

I shut the front door, flicked my outside light to off, turned, and walked back to the kitchen. Once in the kitchen I placed the empty candy bowl on the counter near the microwave. My popcorn bag sat, un-popped, inside the microwave. I punched in the minutes on the key pad and stood waiting for magic to occur. The sweet, buttery smell of popcorn soon filled the kitchen with its welcoming aroma. Ding! The microwave announced its job was finished. It was finished popping the kernels just in time for the start of the evening's horror flick marathon. I dumped the bag of popped kernels into a large bowl, tossed the empty bag into the trash, and headed into the living room. I had waited all day in anticipation of this evening, as it was my single-life tradition to curl up on the couch alone and cower under a fleece blanket while I watched the season's last horror movie lineup. Tomorrow would make tonight's horror fest a bittersweet memory that I could put away in the vault until next Halloween, when the fun could begin again.

I made my way across the hardwood floor to my well-worn, brown leather couch and plopped down with butterflies fluttering like crazy in my stomach. I reached for my blanket that lay on the back of the couch, swung my feet up, covered up, grabbed the remote off the arm, and clicked the TV on. I know it sounds a little nutty, but I just couldn't wait to see the movie lineup for the night. An eerie glow came from the orange Halloween lights I had strung up on my mantel over the fireplace last week. It added to the ambiance of the occasion. I would worry about cleaning up the creepy fake spider webs on the porch banister tomorrow. Everyone had gone home, and all my candy was gone, save one package of Reese's cups I had kept for myself on my kitchen counter. I made a mental note to devour them sometime before bedtime.

Mr. Pickles, my black-and-white cat, was curled up at the one end of the couch near my feet. His soft mewing, as he slept, was comforting to hear while I indulged my wicked side with scary B movies. Tonight's fright fest included several horror classics, but my favorite genres are anything with vampires and werewolves. I don't really care for the gory mummy or zombie movies because they always seem to be a little over the top with their graphics. Give me a good seventies or eighties horror flick with blood that looks fake, and I'm happy as a clam.

After several clicks on my remote, I found a decent Dracula movie from the seventies. I chose the appropriate channel and began what I thought would be a spooky evening with Mr. Pickles and myself. Nothing can ever prepare you for a supernatural encounter, especially if you are not a believer, but I warn you that supernatural phenomena are a reality, whether you have had a personal experience or not. Things exist in our world and are a part of our lives whether we acknowledge their presence or choose to ignore them. They aren't going away. I was never a big religious fanatic or a superstitious person, but I have come to realize that there are some things around all of us that we may not understand. We can't see or touch them, but they are there nonetheless.

I was a good hour into my third movie when I dozed off. The clock on the mantel ticked quietly, along with Mr. Pickle's soft snoring, and induced a hypnotic state over me. I awoke with my heart racing in my chest and blood pounding like a hammer in my skull. I had heard a long, low, guttural growl while I slept. It came from behind the TV. I sat bolt upright and blinked my eyelids several times, wiped some sleep away, and tried to focus on the wall behind the TV. The orange glow coming from the Halloween lights that were attached to the fireplace mantel made it possible for me to make out a strange shape hiding behind the TV. The shape came out from behind the TV and circled around and stood in front of it. The shape had evolved from an eerie shadow to a repulsive creature that was furry all over. It had a man's head, but the body of a large wild dog. The fur appeared to be matted, and the odor that emanated from it was that of a cadaver.

"Christina, do you know what you have done?" the creature said to me. His voice sounded deep and raspy, as if he was a haggard old traveler who had walked hundreds of miles without a drop to drink along the way.

As repulsive as the creature was, I found that I couldn't turn away from his gaze. I was frozen in a state of fear. I was sure my eyes were those of a deer captured in the headlights of an oncoming vehicle. I glanced at Mr. Pickles, but he was impervious to the creature and continued in his deep state of sleep.

Do I dare respond? What will happen if I can't speak? What will happen if it attacks me? Will I be able to defend myself? These were the questions that ran rampant in my mind at the time. The only response I could muster was a shake of my head from side to side to convey that I was clueless.

The creature laughed a deep, maniacal laugh and scoffed at me. "When you watch horror films, you inadvertently invite me into your home."

"What?" I managed to squeak out, even though my whole body trembled when I spoke. "I don't understand."

"You open your home and your soul to me when you view ungodly shows, as you have done for many years."

I breathed a gasp of horror and stared transfixed at the creature. I was still trembling at his presence and could see on his manlike face that I was a great amusement to him. I was utterly speechless.

"You and people like you have no clue as to the power that you allow me to wield in your lives because of something as simple as not being reserved in your viewing pleasures." The creature came toward me and stopped. He stood just on the other side of my coffee table and could leap on my body before I even knew what happened, if he wanted. Bile rose in my throat, and panic was flowing through my body like lava being flushed through a lava tube. "Do you know who I am?"

I was afraid to answer. I wanted to scream at him to make him leave, but I just sat like a stone on my couch.

"I am your worst fear. I am the fallen one, and I claim those wayward souls who believe in my lies." The arrogance he used to proclaim himself to me was downright sinister, and I couldn't help but catch my breath in my throat as I realized what he was telling me.

I managed to squeeze my eyelids shut as I told myself he wasn't real, even though in my heart I knew that to be a lie. I opened my eyelids, and to my surprise, the creature was gone, but he had left a horrifying odor of sulfur and death. Tears began to stream down my cheeks, and an overwhelming sadness engulfed me.

I glanced again in my feline friend's direction and told him, "Mommy is going to church this Sunday and no more scary movies for us!" I scratched Mr. Pickles behind his ears as he magically woke up. He arched his back, yawned, and stretched his forepaws in front of himself. My fear released its grasp on me, and I mustered a long sigh of relief. The creature was gone now, and I intended to make my life right and ensure he wouldn't return. I guess I will have to find something better to watch on Halloween.

HOMICIDAL HAIR: PART I

I listened to the familiar clank as I tossed my keys and they hit the table, along with the whisper soft sound of fabric sliding on itself as I dropped my satiny dress coat on the side table in the foyer at the front door. I turned to shut the door and locked the deadbolt, and while turning back around I kicked off my black stilettos under the same side table. I was exhausted. All I could think of was dragging myself upstairs and slipping into a nice hot bath and, when I was done, crawling into bed and sleeping till noon the next day. Tomorrow was my day off, and after a long and hard work week, I needed a break.

I made my way upstairs to my bedroom, and the sound of my bare footsteps on the staircase and across the second-story hardwood floor seemed more like Igor dragging his gimpy leg and clomping around with his other foot instead of a confident and successful attorney making each step full of purpose and power. Arriving at my bedroom doorway, I noticed a luscious floral scent emanating from my dressing table on the opposite wall. Sitting on my table was a beautiful bouquet of mixed flowers ranging from a bubble gum pink to a royal purple, and they were all dressed up with ribbons of lace and satin interwoven into them and romantically perched in a clear crystalline vase.

"How sweet," I said to myself. It must have cost Jeff a fortune. Jeff was my hairstylist's straying husband. I know what you're thinking: I'm a no good whore, right? Well, let me straighten you out! I had been going to Chloe for three years for her to style my hair. The girl was a whiz at whatever I threw her way, and she was a master chemist when it came to her private label hair care products, and Jeff—well, Jeff is not the marrying kind. I pegged him the first time I met him. Jeff is a playboy through and through, and it confounded me how Chloe got him to the altar. Jeff passed himself around more than a tomcat on a night of prowling, and he had had more than his fair share of sampling in my networking circle. Sure, I felt bad, but only for a second. Jeff was not meant to be a one-woman man and he never would be, no matter what clouded-up, fantasy-driven life Chloe dreamed about.

The neutral plush carpeting felt soothing to my feet as I crossed the room to the table and picked up the note card Jeff had left behind. I read the hastily scribbled work of Jeff. *Rachel, I think she knows. Be careful! Jeff.* "Whatever!" I said out loud, to no one in particular. I dropped the note card on the table and made my way into the master bath.

Walking over to the large antique claw-foot tub, I turned on the faucet and waited for the water to be good and hot before I plugged the drain and added bubbles. I forced myself out of my business dress suit and those damned binding pantyhose while I moaned about it. "I swear a manmade them to make me even more miserable in life than I already was." I tossed my clothes over to the wall by my hamper and watched as they landed in a messy pile of fabric. I was just too tired and lazy to throw them in. "I'll get them tomorrow," I said to myself.

Turning toward the opposite wall and walking to a small bar setup I had concocted for my drinking pleasure, I spied my favorite poison: a deep, dark, perfectly aged merlot. Popping the cork and pouring the sweet aromatic liquid into a long-stemmed wineglass, I took a long sip and reveled in the thought that there was nothing like a soothing hot bath with some specialty hair treatment to make me feel more like the goddess that I am. I sneered at the thought of how naive Chloe was and how foolish and weak-minded Jeff was. I was going to hold on to him as my toy until his usefulness ran out.

With the tub brimming with hot water and bubbles, I made my way to the tub and shut the faucet off. I set my wine glass on the floor close to the tub and climbed into my retreat. Sinking into the envelope of sweet relaxation, I dunked my head just below the surface of water and rose up again. Opening the bottle of shampoo, I threw the cap to the floor, poured some shampoo into my hands, and set the bottle into the soap basket that clung to the side of the tub. I worked up a good lather. The scent was a strange and intoxicating floral mixture. Washing my hair with the shampoo made me feel as if I were indulging in a luxurious spa treatment.

"Wait," I softly spoke to myself out loud. "I don't feel quite right." Maybe it was the effects of the wine reaching my head and making me feel a little giddy, but I didn't drink enough to sicken my stomach, and I was beginning to feel real nauseous. My limbs began to get tingly, and my vision blurred slightly. I thought back to what I had eaten throughout the course of the day, but everything I ingested I had prepared myself. Dinner wasn't fair game, since I hadn't had a bite to eat since lunchtime, when I devoured the lunch I had packed myself. I picked up the bottle of shampoo from the soap basket on the side of the tub and moved it back and forth between my hands.

No, she couldn't be that smart and cunning, could she? Of course, whatever it was it wouldn't be listed under the ingredients. Chloe was a lot more twisted than I thought, and she had cooked up something special just for me. I began to lose the feeling in my hands, and the shampoo bottle slipped from my grasp and into the tub water. The thick liquid oozed out of its home and leaked into the bath water, removing traces of poison by dilution.

My head bobbed and slammed into the edge of the tub, and I blacked out right then and there. My body slackened from the blow, and I sank below the waterline.

*****

The morning news was reporting a crazy story about a local attorney dying in her bathtub the night before. The authorities found her body around noon after her employer phoned in her absence from work and insisted the police check her residence in case of foul play.

The pretty blonde anchorwoman with the bad color job stated that this particular attorney had just finished a high-profile case, and more details about her death would be forthcoming as evidence presented itself.

I smiled to myself and announced to the television set, "Karma." I finished off my cup of coffee and headed to the beauty shop for another full day's work.

HOMICIDAL HAIR: PART II

Jeff opened up the large, intricately carved mahogany door to the family mausoleum with some difficulty. The richly colored wood felt smooth and soft to the touch from being polished for the occasion at hand. The weight of the solid wood door combined with rarely used pins in the hinges caused a squeal of protest. Jeff cringed until the door was fully open for him to pass through the doorway. Jeff was relieved to find the building left unlocked and unattended. He had sat in his vehicle outside in the drive and had waited for the groundskeepers to take their all too predictable lunch break at noon. He knew they would most likely be late in returning from the hour-long rest. They would probably be dragging their feet when it came to begin working again, which gave Jeff time to pay his respects and disappear before anyone had seen him.

The mausoleum was a fairly massive structure that had been built in the late 1800s. The ceiling was high in the chapel and had large columns supporting the entrance from the chapel into the crypt area. The nature of the architecture screamed Gothic, and the atmosphere seemed almost magical when one entered into its womb. Even though the air was cool and smelled antiseptic in nature, it did nothing to take away from the grim reminder of death that clung to every bit of the inside of the building. The windows were priceless stained glass that stood the test of time with beauty and elegance. Each window had its own biblical theme situated expertly within its arched molding. The glass seemed to explode with the vibrant shades of a rainbow as the sun shone through the individual panes. It was ethereal.

Jeff slowly walked around the perimeter of the large room, gazing at the nameplates and mounted flower vases that were attached to each occupied tomb. He was halfway around when he encountered the casket waiting eagerly to be placed in its final resting place. Reflecting on his past intimate relationship with the remains of the woman inside, he allowed his right hand to glide over the smooth surface of the lid and admired the money that her family had put into her death. There was never a time in life when rich didn't come in handy for Jeff. Money and privilege were the two most important things to Jeff, and to do without those was simply unacceptable. So when Jeff hooked up with Rachel, an energetic attorney who had paid her dues and was on the rise both professionally and financially, Jeff made sure he road that boat as long as possible. His wife, Chloe, had been oblivious to the affair they had begun and continued for several months. Chloe was a sweet, innocent, hard-working young career woman who had the makings of greatness and just needed Jeff to push her in the right direction, but Jeff had become bored of their intimate and intellectual life and needed some variety to break up the monotony. That is what he found in Rachel's arms. He was going to miss Rachel, but nothing was forever, and he had other prospects he could dial up and latch onto until the time came to toss them away and move on.

Jeff's thoughts came back to the present, and he glanced at his watch and decided to get the lead out and get moving. When Jeff had originally entered the building he had assumed that he would be leaving at some point, but he was wrong.

*****

A dark figure lurked in the shadows of the mausoleum. The figure was watching and waiting for the right time to do what they had come for. Scrunched up against a marbled wall in the far corner of the crypt, hidden by ominous shadows, the figure held in a gasp as a well-built, middle-aged man came onto the scene. The very person the figure had been expecting to arrive was unaware of their presence, but in due time the man would rue the day they had ever crossed paths. The plot had already been formed, and all that needed to happen was to play out the final scene.

The figure wore dark colors, as expected. Black skid-free shoes, black sweat jacket with the hood drawn up, black jeans, and last but not least, black gloves. The gloves were a last-minute decision. Getting caught was the least of the figure's worries, but one could not be too cautious, could they? The perpetrator of the impending crime watched Jeff walk along the eastern wall and trace his fingers over each and every name placard.

*****

Absorbed in his actions, Jeff failed to notice the coffin sitting near an opening in the wall, where it would be interred after the groundskeepers came back from their lunch break. He practically fell over the coffin after running into it, but quickly regained his footing at the last second. Jeff was startled at first when he righted himself but then was relieved, because this casket was the one he had expected to be already entombed in its final resting place.

Jeff tenderly ran his hand over the top of the casket, bent closer, and whispered a private message to the occupant through the lid. Jeff straightened his posture; smoothed out his business jacket, and turned to leave—but not before his skull was struck from his right side, which caused his body to collapse to the cold stone floor in excruciating pain. Blackness engulfed him as the blow reverberated throughout his entire body.

*****

With time to spare, the dark figure opened up the coffin's two lids, dragged Jeff's unconscious body over to it, and struggled under the weight to place him inside. After several minutes of struggling and a lot of sweating, Jeff was deposited on top of the casket's corpse and the lid was shut. Because two bodies were now inside the coffin, the killer had to use force to close the lid until it latched. With a sigh of relief, the dark figure began the clean-up process, making good use of a nearby bucket and mop that the groundskeepers conveniently left out before leaving for their break. With the blood droplets and small puddles mopped up and the urn put back where it belonged, the killer exited the building in a quick fashion, being careful to peel away their outer layer of clothing, shoving it into a bag to dispose of later and revealing street clothes to wear for the escape. There was about fifteen more minutes until the workers returned, giving the floor time to dry and the killer time to leave unnoticed.

*****

Chloe's husband Jeff hadn't made it home last night, and she rose early in the morning to report him missing. She wasn't too concerned about him being out late, but since he hadn't arrived home and the sun was up, the situation changed. She had made several attempts at phoning his cell, friends, and family to no avail, which left her no choice but to telephone the authorities. Chloe's hands shook as she dialed the numbers and waited for someone to answer. After she spoke with a detective, Chloe hung up and whispered to herself, "Karma is a killer."

UNTIL FOREVER

Waves of rage crashed into the cliffs that were positioned below my bedroom window. The water gave a brutal lashing to the rocky outcropping and was relentless in its announcement of hierarchy in nature. The thunderous roaring of sea water left me speechless and enthralled every time the earth was blessed with another wave. The cool air signaled an end to the summer and the beginning of fall, and the taste of salt was becoming thicker in the sea spray that made it to my tongue.

I looked out the arched stained glass that allowed the sun's golden rays of warmth in with an explosion of brilliant colors and gave thanks for the beautiful residence and its majestic splendor that lent to the mystical atmosphere. I wrapped my shawl around my shoulders a little tighter than usual, so the warmth would give way to a feeling of safety and love. The spire that I inhabited was a magical place of peace and beauty. It was a fairytale-princess spire that seemed to reach up to heaven and caress its underbelly. The old stonework and the pointed roof told its age, but the solidity of its innards spoke volumes about its longevity.

I can't remember a time when I was ever happier. My husband lay sleeping peacefully in our bed, and as I turned from the window to watch his sweet slumber, I couldn't help but be warmed by his nudging of my pillow's corner as he tossed toward where I should've been lying. The warmth of my body still clung to the bedclothes, and his body sought my form out, but to no avail. His eyelids opened, and he smiled a sleepy smile and patted the spot beside him where I belonged. I strolled over to the bedside, tossed my wrap onto the floor, slipped into bed, and snuggled peacefully into his loving embrace.

Noon came and went, but we still did not stir from our bedchamber. I knew that tonight would be the night my love would leave me all alone and travel the seaside in search of his identity. You see, it would be a full moon, and nighttime would end my bliss and begin his terror. He would creep into the countryside and stalk his prey, and when he was satiated he would return to me until the next full moon. The outer townsfolk knew his cycle all too well and had learned to be scarce on his nights of prowling. I have also learned, all too well, to love him as much as I can, and to give him over to his curse so he can come back, renewed, into my open embrace. Our love was greater than his curse, and one fine day we would both be free, but until then I would trust that his great love for us would carry him through.

*****

My love's body shivers with delight as I caress his inner thighs. He turns to me, and we make passionate love on the very eve of his physical transformation. I will not see his re-creation because he will have fled our spire's bed before he has metamorphosed. My safety and the safety of those around us is his utmost concern. He will lock himself into a self-built holding cell until his transformation is complete, and then he will be loosed and troll the land until dawn.

My lover's caress ends with an explosion of deep satisfaction. He opens his eyes and tells me he loves me and crawls from our bed. It is now past two in the afternoon, and my husband walks to the window and closes it with purpose. He turns and gazes at me with hunger written in his eyes. I know that look as the look of an animal who cannot be satisfied with its prey until every morsel has been consumed. Sadness engulfs his features, and I am saddened as well. His sorrow has etched a permanent mark on my soul, and no amount of love can ever erase it. An overwhelming feeling of grief takes hold of me as he dresses for his evening. He kisses my forehead—the kiss of the undead— opens the Gothic, solid wooden door, and leaves me in a weeping mess as I throw myself onto the bed.

In a crumpled, helpless heap I sob uncontrollably and soak the bed with our shame, washing away the love that had been made just a few moments before. When I have finished with the onslaught of tears, I rise from our bed to start a fire in the hearth. I strike a match and throw it onto the leftover lumber from the night before. The wood is well weathered and dry all the way through. It lights easily, and I begin to prepare my bath for the coming evening alone.

I make my way to the linen's resting place, a well-worn wooden rack that displays our bath towels just inside the doorway to our master bath. I carefully choose my towel and place it on a chaise beside the antique claw-foot tub. The towel is lavender in color and fragrance and gives off a calming aroma. I remove a bottle containing a bath liquid from a basket beside the tub and pour its contents into the cold iron belly. I turn the silver-plated faucets to the on position, adjust the water temperature accordingly, and watch as the water gives birth to the bubbles.

My heart is heavy with sadness as I climb into the bubbling warmth. I sink into the tub until just the top of my head and nose remain above the water. I raise my face toward the ceiling and tilt my head back to saturate my hair with the water's warmth. I sit upright and remove a homemade oatmeal soap bar from the basket attached to the rim of the tub. I lather my whole body with the soap. I begin by washing my face, neck, and shoulders; when I reach my breasts, I caress each one carefully and move on to my stomach. I reach for my bath brush and lather the soap onto it and begin scrubbing my back. I rinse the brush and return it to its home and lather up my legs and feet. Then I dunk down to rinse, splashing some of the life-giving liquid onto the floor. After rinsing my body, I rise to lather and wash my female parts, and then I squat down and rinse my body again. I replace the soap bar and retrieve the shampoo from the same basket and pour some of its contents into my palm. I rub the luxurious liquid into my hair and cleanse away the past and make my body fresh for a new day coming. I dunk back down into the water to rinse my hair, and then return to the surface. I lean back against the tub and allow my eyelids to take a rest and close for a spell. I fall asleep in the soothing hydrosphere until an unnatural howling pierces the air with its song of remorse, signaling my husband's transformation and escape to the outside world.

My eyelids pop open, and my heart begins its race; its beating becomes erratic, and simultaneously my adrenaline skyrockets. I don't want to panic. I must calm down. My love will again take me into his embrace, and we will be whole again. I am not complete apart from him, and he is not complete apart from me. Oh, how my heart aches for his gentle touch, and my delicate flower quivers in anticipation of his return. He is my sun, my moon, and my twinkling stars, and I am his sparkling diamond, polished like glass. My eyes are the purest of crystalline mated with sapphire irises, and my love can see our future when he gazes into them.

I slowly crawl from the bath and dry my body with the towel, and I then wrap it around my naked form and lie on the chaise to wait for my husband. Our bedroom door swings open wide just as dawn approaches, and his dark form stands erect in the doorway. I can smell his animalistic nature, raw and unnatural. He begs me to release him from the curse and hands me a hunting bow loaded with a single arrow made from the finest silver in the land. His body is coated with the blood of his prey, and his demeanor is that of a scared little boy. I move from the chaise to his side to embrace his guilt. We cling to each other and kiss the kiss of love and desperation. I can taste fear on his tongue. Our mouths part and he releases from our embrace. Backing away from me, he holds out his arms, closes his eyelids, and tilts his head back in silence. A single tear slips from his right eye and slides down his cheek. He waits for me.

My heart begins to race erratically again, and my mind spins at his request. I raise the bow and aim the arrow at his heart. I pause. An onslaught of silent tears begins to flow from my eyes and down my cheeks, soaking my skin in sorrow with each rivulet. He stands still, waiting for me. I squeeze my eyes shut and remember the love we have and the passion we live for and the fire in our touch. I pull the trigger and the arrow drives its way to the intended target, and my love drops to the floor, dead. My sorrow engulfs me, and I run to his lifeless form and sob over him. His skin begins to cool as I collapse onto the floor beside him.

How can I endure a life without my husband? I will no longer feel his loving arms wrapped around me in rapture, nor will he gaze into my eyes and seek out my soul for his taking. Pleasure in life holds no meaning for me now. My love is gone. His curse has ended, but mine has just begun.

I rise from my husband's side and put away my fear and sadness for the moment. Above the mantle in our bedroom hangs a dagger made for a time like this time. I walk to the dagger's home and retrieve it from the wall. I make my way back to my love's lifeless form and fall to my knees, naked. I raise the dagger into the air with both hands and drive it as hard as I can into my chest. The blade plunges stealthily into my heart.

Love will endure this tragedy, and we will rise to a new day.

NO MEANS NO

I picked up the poker that leaned precariously in its holder and pushed around some coal, along with the last log in the stone fireplace. I could hear Jaimeson Fontaine walking down the hallway toward his office, where I was waiting for his instructions. His walk was full of purpose, and before I even saw his presence in the doorway, I knew that tonight would end badly. Jaimeson had made many physical passes at me in the past, and I believe I had put him off long enough and he wasn't going to tolerate waiting any longer. I was going to announce my resignation tonight, and I knew Jaimeson was going to fight with me about it. I had told George, the butler, earlier in the day about my plan to leave. George and I were of the same mind. He promised he wouldn't be far from Jaimeson's office should I need his help. George had witnessed many advances that Jaimeson had made in the past on his other assistants and knew that by his nature, anything that did not result in him getting his way would end badly.

Jaimeson pushed open the door and stared hard at me from across the room. It was a cold stare without one ounce of emotion. He turned and shut the door behind him, and I flinched at the sound. He strode over to where I stood by the fireplace with the poker still in my hand, and he relieved me of my weapon and tossed it across the room. My breath quickened and my heart started pounding in my chest as Jaimeson reached out to me with his hand. I put my right hand in his, and he pulled me hard into his embrace.

"Oh, Claudia," he breathed into my hair. "I have waited for this moment all day." He separated from me just enough to look into my eyes with his penetrating gaze. "Please don't turn me down today." His grip on my hand increased when I didn't respond immediately. I winced in pain, and he released my hand but still held me face-to-face with our bodies touching in a provocative manner.

"Jaimeson, really!" I half laughed, trying to lighten the air up a bit. "I have told you before I wasn't interested. I want a business relationship only." He balked at the rejection as if I had injured him.

Jaimeson gave me his boyish smirk and shoved me against the wall hard and kissed me fervently. I can't say that it didn't affect me, but he was a user and an abuser, and I didn't want to be mixed up with him on a personal level. Then again, what girl doesn't want a handsome, take-charge, rich significant other? It was a turn-on to be physically manhandled in the sack a little, but I wasn't up for the mental and emotional abuse in a relationship that I knew he would dish out. When he was done, I would be tossed aside for his next flavor of the month. I tried to push Jaimeson off, but he wasn't having it. His right hand began caressing my cheek, and then he snaked his fingers up into my hair, giving it a good yank. His kiss traveled a path down my neck as his left hand slid up under my skirt. I was throbbing with desire inside, but my heart wouldn't let go of my pride.

"Enough!" I said as I pushed Jaimeson as hard as I could. He lost his grip and seemed taken aback by my forcefulness. "I'm done," I urgently blurted out. The shock that registered on his face was disconcerting. "I've had enough, and I am resigning tonight." I poised myself in a stiff stance to show I meant business. "I would normally give a notice, but since the circumstances are what they are, I'm leaving tonight."

Jaimeson raised his eyebrows, and a devilish grin formed on his lips. He released his embrace and backed up from me.

"I'm glad I amuse you, but I'm serious!" I didn't see it coming. Three slaps landed hard across my face and about knocked me to the floor. I would have fallen, but the wall saw to it to keep me from that type of disaster. My face stung, and I literally saw stars. Bright little flashes were going off in my eyesight as I slid down the wall. Everything went blurry, and then I went out cold.

I awoke to a dragging noise near the doorway. I blinked my eyelids open and tried to clear my head. Sitting up and leaning against the wall, I saw two legs in dress pants attached to two feet in dress shoes slide out the doorway, leaving a trail of crimson. I heard a few more doors open and close, and then silence. It seemed like eons before I heard footsteps coming down the hall toward the office, where I sat against the wall in stunned silence. My mind was in a fog, and I was trying hard to regain my composure.

"Miss Claudia, are you OK?" George said as he poked his head inside the doorway.

"Yes, George. I will be." I tried to slide myself back up the wall. George came through the doorway and helped me to stand. I hugged him hard. He was my savior. "Thank you, George," I whispered in his ear.

"You're welcome, Miss Claudia." Things were a little fuzzy at the moment, but my head was beginning to clear up a bit. I released George from our embrace and quizzically looked at him.

"Miss Claudia, I couldn't bear for Mr. Fontaine to hurt you any further than he has. I try to keep to myself and be a good employee, but enough is enough." I nodded at George in agreement. "We must get rid of the body."

My heart pounded at the thought of Jaimeson's fate. Was this really happening? Maybe I hit my head on something and this was all a dream. I began to panic, but I nodded again in agreement and followed George as he headed out of the office and down the main hallway to the kitchen. I continued to follow George into the kitchen and out the side door. There, at the back of Jaimeson's limousine, lay his body, already wrapped up in black plastic and awaiting transportation. George positioned himself at Jaimeson's head and I at his feet. We bent over at the same time and heaved Jaimeson's body up and into the trunk. George looked at me wearily and dangled keys from his hand as he walked to the driver's-side door. The jangling noise had no sense of comfort to it. Even though my tormentor was gone, I would still have to live with these actions for the rest of my life. I walked to the passenger side of the limo and climbed in.

"Miss Claudia, you should sit in the back. It would look odd to others if you were in the front with me," George said matter-of-factly. I nodded in agreement and did as I was told. My head was still reeling from the attack, and I wasn't in the frame of mind to argue. I exited the passenger side and walked to the back of the limo, where George was magically waiting for me with the door open. I smiled at George and crawled inside. Once inside, I lay down on the long seat and closed my eyelids for a bit. I heard the car switch from park to drive and then heard the familiar sound of the tires riding on the brick driveway. It was quite some time before we came to a complete stop. I sat up in the seat and peered out the long window on the side of the vehicle. George exited the car and came around to open the door for me. After George opened the door and I stepped out, I noticed that we were at the back of Jaimeson's property, a heavily wooded area that was far removed from the manor.

"Help me with the body," George said. I walked to the rear of the vehicle and, in the same manner we had put Jaimeson in the trunk, we took him out and placed his body on the ground. Pine trees were the main attraction here, and the smell of pine was familiar and comforting. I shivered at the breeze that came in from the west and swirled through the trees. I rubbed my arms with my hands to stamp out the goose bumps that arose. After removing a shovel from the trunk, George began to dig a deep hole in the ground about ten feet from where we were parked. The ground was flat in that area and the rains that had come in the past two days had made it easy for George to accomplish his task. It seemed like forever and a day before the hole was finished. George tossed aside the shovel and walked back to where I stood at the trunk. He motioned for me to help him lift Jaimeson's body. I bent to pick up Jaimeson's feet, and then we simultaneously stood and carried the body over to the hole and dropped him in.

"George, how will we explain this?" I stared into the black of the hole and then looked up to look George in the eye.

George shrugged his shoulders. "You will leave, and we will never speak again. I will tell others that Mr. Fontaine has taken an indefinite sabbatical." I raised my eyebrows in disbelief. George went on. "After a bit of time has passed, I will then inform others that Mr. Fontaine has come under a most unfortunate climbing accident and died while making his way up a remote mountainside somewhere. I can figure out the details between now and the time of the fictitious accident."

"George, I'm not so sure this will work." I was now biting my lip in guilt and in panic, but somehow George's demeanor kept me from going over the edge. George bent down to retrieve the shovel and began shoveling dirt back into the hole to cover up our crime.

"Miss Claudia, we have to make it work." George continued to shovel, and when he was finished he walked over to the trunk and tossed the shovel in and closed the door. He began to brush off his clothes and saw the distressed look on my face. He encircled his arms in a friendly manner around my shoulders and guided me to the passenger door. "Everything will be OK."

I slid into the open door and down the long seat, alone. The car door closed, and George got in the driver's seat. He started the limo and put it in drive.

*****

The plane shuddered a few times, and I gripped my seat a little tighter as the nose tipped up toward the heavens. The plane evened out, and we were well on our way to sanctuary. Anywhere but back there is where I wanted to be. Even with the occasional jarring of the plane, due to turbulence, my nerves were much better off than on the ground.

I sat alone in my row and hiked up the right side of my skirt to look at the bruise that I knew was growing like a fungus. It had already begun to turn purple immediately after Jaimeson had pinned me against the wall at the office two hours earlier. I snaked my fingers up into my hair and felt for the lump on the back of my head that, I was sure, was the size of an orange. I had collapsed after the few blows that Jaimeson had dealt me, along with the fall to the floor. If it hadn't been for the adrenaline that coursed through my veins and a little help from George, I would have never made it to the plane.

"Miss, would you like a soda?" The stewardess pointed to the top shelf of her cart. Startled, I extracted my fingers from my hair and dropped my hand to my lap. She looked like the typical girl next door: blonde, blue-eyed, and about a size zero with the features of an angel. The bright blue uniform she wore made my eyes scream in pain. I kept looking at the cart shelf as she rattled off what was available. I took what seemed like an eon to make my choice. "I'd like a diet cola, please." Her look of disdain at my delay in answering her only heightened my irritation at her interruption. I popped the tab on the can as the stewardess walked another row up. Looking down at my leg, I pushed slightly on my bruise and winced in pain. I took a sip of pop, set my can down in the cup holder, and rose to take a bathroom break. I walked down the narrow aisle of the plane and made it to the bathroom. I opened the door and entered the tiny cocoon. I was greeted by a large mirror that hung on the wall above the small sink basin. I stared hard at my reflection. I was slightly disheveled in appearance, but I looked better than I felt. My whole body ached, and my mind was reeling after the evening's horrible events. Just as I bent to remove my panties and sit to relieve myself, a flash in the mirror caught my eye. I stood straight up, looked up and into the mirror again, and I saw a familiar face. Horrified, I turned quickly to look behind me, but there was no one behind me. I sat hard on the toilet and gripped my chest in pain. I finished my business on the toilet and rose to pull up my panties. After doing so, I stood straight up and glanced in the mirror again.

To my horror, there was Jaimeson looking back at me for the second time. I saw that his hand rested on my shoulder, and I actually felt it gripping my flesh. I turned around and was greeted by his dead, grinning face.

"Hello, Claudia."

A HARD LESSON LEARNED

Jodie arrived at the hospital in her pajamas and tennis shoes. Her hair was disheveled, but she didn't care. Jodie's ex-husband had called her just after midnight with the news that their daughter, Shayla, had been admitted to the local hospital for domestic violence injuries. Jodie had jumped out of bed after hanging up, slipped on her tennis shoes, and dashed out of the house without brushing her hair or changing into street clothes.

Jodie arrived at the hospital fifteen minutes after leaving her home, parked her car, walked to the front, and entered by passing through a large revolving door. Her gait was hurried as she went straight to the information desk. The air was sterile, and the old lobby furniture, with its stained seats and tattered edges, was long overdue to be replaced. The decor of the walls reminded Jodie of elementary school with its glossy maize-colored paint and brown tiled walls. It felt more like a sanitarium than a hospital. The appearance of the old, matronly looking woman behind the desk wasn't much better than Jodie's. Her hair was twisted in a French knot that looked like it hadn't been washed for a good month or two, and her frumpy, outdated clothing was too tight for her obese body. Jodie expected the receptionist to give her a hard time, but when Jodie stepped up to the counter and the woman greeted Jodie, she must have recognized a mother in need. She promptly retrieved Shayla's information from the database and instructed Jodie where to go.

Jodie hurriedly made her way to the elevators, pushed the arrow up button, and waited impatiently for the doors to open and beckon her in. The elevator arrived within a few moments, the doors opened, and Jodie entered and turned around. While waiting for the doors to close, she pushed button number three and contemplated Shayla's relationship with her boyfriend. Shayla's boyfriend, Justin, had finally done it. He had put her through hell this past year, and after many pleadings from her parents and months of abuse from Justin, Shayla left him. Jodie knew that is what put Justin over the edge. He had threatened Shayla and her family with violence before, and he had finally made good on part of his threat. The elevator doors closed, and it worked its way upward. The elevator made the familiar ding for each floor it passed and then quickly stopped at number three. The doors opened, and Jodie felt a humongous weight being put on her shoulders. She could barely take the first step out of the elevator doors for fear of what she would find when she saw Shayla. Once out of the elevator, Jodie made her way down a long corridor and passed a nurses' station while eyeing the room numbers beside each doorway. She arrived at Shayla's room and took a deep breath before pushing the heavy door open and walking inside.

Shayla lay on the window side of the room. Her body was covered to her waist with a plain white hospital blanket. The bed was elevated and slightly raised her head. Her body was still, and her breathing seemed even and not labored. Shayla's face was bandaged just above her left eye, and her right cheek bore the bruising and swelling associated with a strong backhanded blow. Anger bubbled inside of Jodie, and she dared not let it loose at the present. All she wanted was for Shayla to come out of this with no permanent damage and a hard lesson learned. Jodie saw the bruising that striped Shayla's arms and it was all she could do to contain herself. She walked over to Shayla's bedside and sat down quietly so she didn't disturb her daughter's slumber. A few moments later, a doctor softly knocked on Shayla's door and popped her head in.

"Mrs. Carson?" The question irritated Jodie immensely, but she didn't show it. Carson was her former married name, and the doctor would not have known that Jodie had it changed to her maiden name after the divorce, so she disregarded the last name and answered.

"I'm Shayla's mother, Jodie," she replied with heaviness in her voice. She shifted in her seat as the doctor motioned for her to come out into the hall. Jodie acquiesced to her request and stood up, walked over to the door, and went into the hall. She softly shut the door behind her and waited for the doctor to speak.

The doctor, Dr. Barone, was a short, middle-aged woman who had kindness in her eyes. She seemed to share the heaviness that Jodie did over Shayla's injuries and eased Jodie's mind when she went over the extent of the physical damage. "There were no internal injuries to her organs, a good amount of bruising here and there on her arms and legs, along with some contusions to the face. The open wound over her eye will scar very little after the stitches have healed." She seemed quite pleased with her assessment. "She'll heal up just fine in a few weeks and will be able to go home in the morning." The doctor sighed and moved her weight from one foot to the next and back again, as if she had to use the ladies' room, so Jodie thanked her and quickly returned to Shayla's bedside.

Shayla was still fast asleep. Jodie didn't stay much longer because the longer she stayed, the more her anger grew, and she needed an outlet. Twenty minutes after the doctor spoke to her, Jodie decided now was the time to make things right. She knew her decision would probably put her behind bars, but it was better than Shayla or some other girl being injured down the road, and she couldn't live with that guilt hanging over her head unless she tried to do something about the situation. Justin had made a grave mistake, and it was going to cost him dearly in the end. Jodie was going to make him pay for his crime because she knew that the law would only slap him on the hand and send him on his merry way to abuse someone else, if not go after Shayla again, and Jodie wasn't having it. She couldn't take the chance. Jodie mulled it over and told herself it was a mother's job to protect her children no matter what the cost, and that was exactly what she intended to do.

Jodie rose from her chair next to Shayla's bedside, placed a kiss gingerly on her left cheek, and walked out of the room. Jodie made it to the elevators quite rapidly. She pushed the down button on the wall and waited. Her nervous toe tapping didn't speed up the elevator's progress, but she was relieved when she heard the ding announcing its arrival and watched the doors open. She entered the elevator and pushed the lobby button and the doors closed. The elevator was quick to drop to her intended floor and spit her back out into the lobby for her to leave. Jodie exited the hospital and started formulating her next action. She had to go home and change her clothes. She decided dark clothing would be best, and she would need some equipment for the task that lay before her.

By the time Jodie pulled in her drive, she had become quite lucid in her thought process and mechanical in her movements. Her plan was completely formulated when she finally put the car in park and hopped out, slamming the door shut. The slam echoed in the garage and made Jodie cringe. She hated that sound. It was the all-too-familiar sound that her ex made when he came home angry every day from work. His work life had been very stressful and, to the detriment of his marriage, he had brought it home with him consistently.

Jodie fumbled with her house keys and stuck the appropriate key in the deadbolt and unlocked the kitchen door. She was greeted with emptiness. Living alone was still strange to Jodie after ten years of divorce. She never got used to the quiet or the chill that never left the air, even if the thermostat was turned up past seventy degrees. Jodie entered the kitchen and went straight to the linen closet. Each step she took on the bare hardwood floor made a hollow clopping noise as she progressed down the hallway. After reaching the closet door, Jodie opened it and pulled the light switch string and immediately set to work foraging in boxes to gather necessary items to complete her mission.

Jodie managed to find her bag of cotton balls, her microwaveable hot wax kit, which included wax, linen strips, and all the necessary products to complete a successful wax service. Jodie placed all the items into an empty box she found tucked under the bottom shelf. She pulled the light string and paused as it sprang upward and clinked against the light base and dropped back down. Jodie pushed the door closed, picked up her box, and headed for her bedroom to change into something a little more inconspicuous. Jodie flicked on her bedroom light and placed her box of goodies on her bed. Jodie turned and went to her dresser at the foot of her bed and rummaged around for her clothing. She pulled a pair of dark jeans from her jean drawer, a black T-shirt from the drawer below, and retrieved a pair of dark, soft-soled boots from beside her dresser. Jodie sat on her bed with a sigh and began to change out of her pajamas and into her criminal attire. Jodie finished her transformation quickly and rose from the bed, picked up her box, switched out the light, and headed for the kitchen to claim a pair of scissors and some duct tape from her buffet.

Once in the kitchen, Jodie scrounged around her buffet's top drawer and found the scissors and tape. Before retrieving the items, her hand grazed an old school photo of Shayla from her third-grade year. Jodie reached for the picture and allowed her mind to travel back in time to when Shayla was nine years old and remember how innocent and full of life her little girl had been. She placed the photo back in the drawer and came back to reality. Jodie hadn't seen her daughter full of life for a very long time. Justin had managed to extinguish the light in Shayla's eyes and squash her adventurous spirit. Jodie's heart was hurting at her present thoughts, and she vowed to avenge her daughter and give Justin a lesson he will never forget.

Jodie finished up her hunting and gathering and made her way to the garage again, walked around to the trunk, and opened the hatch. She quickly dropped her items into the trunk of her car. Slamming the trunk lid down, Jodie stopped to think a moment about what she was really getting herself into. While prison was a good probability, guilt over the actions she was prepared to take would be non-existent. The consequences were not something that Jodie was willing to concentrate too much on; at this point, it didn't matter. Justin deserved what was about to be dealt to him, and let the cards fall where they may afterwards. Jodie shook her head to clear it and opened the driver's-side door and hopped into the seat. The engine roared to life as she turned the key in the ignition. Jodie put the car in reverse and backed out. Once she cleared the garage door, she hit the automatic door button and watched the garage door come down and proceeded to back out of her drive rather quickly.

Adrenaline was kicking in, and Jodie's heart was starting to race in anticipation of the events that were about to unfold. It was all she could do to keep her speed at the legal limit. Jodie was ready to get the mission over with, wash her hands of it, and help Shayla move on. It only took Jodie fifteen minutes to drive from her house to Justin's. Jodie was amazed that she had even made it without a being stopped for a number of traffic violations that she had committed with all the speeding and weaving in and out of traffic that she did, and the few lights she went through that happened to turn red just as she was about to pass under.

Jodie noticed as she pulled up to the neat little ranch home that all the lights were out and Justin's car was in the drive. Jodie slowed her pace and gingerly pulled her car into the drive behind Justin's revamped 1985 Chevy Camaro. That car was his pride and joy, and Jodie wondered as she turned off her car engine what he would think if she attacked his vehicle instead of him. No; Jodie quickly shifted her mind's gears back to Justin needing to feel some physical consequences for what he had done to her Shayla, and Jodie was more determined than ever to accomplish just that. By the actions that she was about to embark on, Jodie believed that whatever the outcome, Shayla would benefit. Justin would probably take one of two routes: break up with Shayla for good and have herself thrown in jail, or straighten himself out and treat her better. Either way, it was a win-win situation for

Shayla. At least that was what Jodie convinced herself of.

Jodie climbed out of her car and went to the trunk to extract her instruments of revenge and made her way to the front door. Walking along the sidewalk in front of the house, Jodie remembered that Justin kept a spare key to the front door underneath the seat of a decorative stool he had sitting beside the door against the siding of the house. Jodie focused on the house numbers attached to the siding, and then her eyes wandered down to the stool where the key was hidden. She stooped over and set her box down, reached for the stool, picked it up, turned it over, and pulled the key out from a pocket of wood that Justin had glued to the bottom. Jodie straightened herself, put the key in the keyhole, turned the key, turned the knob, opened the door, picked up her box, and entered the snake pit.

The house was completely dark except for a tiny light coming from the bathroom night-light down the hallway. The odor of the house hadn't changed much since the last time Jodie had been inside. The beer and cigarettes still overwhelmed the atmosphere with their presence. Jodie could her Justin snoring from somewhere down the hallway. She knew that his bedroom was the last door on the left, and she made her way as quickly as she could to Justin's door with her box of goodies in tow.

Jodie paused at Justin's doorway. Justin's door was wide open, and the smell of beer was the strongest here. Jodie was sickened to her stomach and tasted stomach acid at the back of her throat. She swallowed hard, trying not to bring up her dinner—or anything else, for that matter. Jodie stepped through the doorway and quietly walked toward Justin's bed. Jodie waited a few moments for her eyes to adjust better to the darkness, and she then placed her box down on the carpet beside the bed. Peering down at his sleeping form, Jodie swallowed hard again and set about her work. She poked at Justin's shoulder a couple of times to make sure he was really out, and then reached down to open up her box after she was satisfied with Justin's non-movement. Jodie opened her box and pulled out the duct tape. Climbing on top of the bed and straddling Justin, to her disgust she noticed that he was only wearing a pair of loose-fitting boxers. She began to tape around Justin's left wrist. Then she stretched his arm toward the headboard, wrapped the tape around the bedpost several times to secure it, and broke off the end. Jodie proceeded to do the same to his right wrist, pausing for a moment when Justin began to stir. All Jodie kept telling herself was to get done quickly: secure Justin to his bed, silence him with one of his socks, and then she would be free to do whatever she wanted to do to him. Justin stopped moving, and Jodie finished securing his right wrist with the tape to the other bedpost. Jodie then carefully crawled off of Justin's sleeping form, crawled to the bottom of the bed, and set about securing his ankles. She did the same to his ankles that she did to his wrists and crept off of the bed and went to his dresser drawer across from the end of the bed. Quietly she opened the top right drawer and found what she was looking for. Jodie pulled a clean sock from the drawer and smiled in anticipation of what she was about to do next. Jodie pushed the drawer shut and turned to face the bed again. She crept back onto the mattress and straddled Justin's body once again. With a smile on her face, Jodie balled up the sock and shoved it into Justin's open mouth.

Justin began to cough and gag and thrash about. The only thing he accomplished was upsetting Jodie and tilting her to one side, which she quickly recovered from. Justin struggled against the tape securing his limbs and tried to spit out the sock, to no avail. Jodie reached over to the nightstand and turned on the lamp. Justin's eyelids squinted as he tried to focus on the intruder. When he was able to focus his drunken gaze a bit, he had shock written on his face.

"Well, Justin," Jodie grinned. "You have been a very bad, bad boy tonight." Justin's eyelids opened wider, which made Jodie grin even more. "Momma is going to teach you a lesson."

Jodie climbed off of Justin and the bed. She stood, and then stooped down to open her box of goodies and pull out the pair of scissors she had brought. Jodie waved the scissors back and forth in front of Justin's face and watched the fear set in. Justin's body began to buck wildly. He couldn't accomplish much, because Jodie made sure that he was fastened snugly to the headboard and footboard. After a few minutes of wriggling, Justin's body ceased its dance and he relaxed a bit, but Jodie knew he was only resting up for another struggle.

"This will be an easy job for me tonight." Jodie stopped the scissor waving and began to cut away his boxers. The underwear was all Justin had on, and it was going to make Jodie's job easier. She decided that she was going to start with Justin's chest and make her way down his stomach and on to his scrotum. "This is going to hurt you more than it will me." Jodie tried to squelch a giggle unsuccessfully. Justin began his wriggle waltz again. Jodie stood beside the bed and waited for Justin to calm down a bit. He tired quickly and relaxed again, and Jodie resumed her job of cutting off the boxers. After the final cut was complete, Justin's boxers fell to either side and presented his manhood to Jodie.

Justin tried spitting out the sock and wriggling again, but his efforts were futile. Jodie saw the rage in his eyes and knew that if he got free that she would be his next victim, and Jodie would be damned if that was going to happen. If she got the snot beat out of her, she was going to finish her job first and pay for it later. She had no intention of undoing Justin's bound limbs and decided early on that he would have to manage to get them off on his own somehow, later.

Jodie set the scissors back in the box and retrieved the wax container. It took only a few moments for Jodie to take the wax to the kitchen, heat it up, and return to the bedroom. To Justin, it seemed a lifetime before Jodie reappeared. Jodie entered the bedroom and set the wax on the nightstand and picked up the package of linen strips from the kit. Jodie opened the package in a hurried fashion and laid out numerous strips on the edge of the nightstand. Jodie placed the remaining strips back into her wax kit and pulled out the scissors and began cutting linen into the appropriate lengths needed to get the wax job done. Actually, Jodie didn't need to cut the strips; she just wanted to drag out the process and set Justin on edge a little bit more. His eyelids were wide with knowing what was about to happen and that he was not in a position to stop it. Jodie occasionally glanced at Justin's face and reveled in the fact that he was going to be a very sorry, sad little man very soon.

Jodie finished preparing the wax strips and lined them up by size along the edge of the nightstand. Jodie then reached down and pulled out few Popsicle sticks and set them on the nightstand as well. "We better get working, or the wax is going to cool too much and I will have to heat it again." Jodie watched as Justin raised his eyebrows in terror. Justin resumed his wild wriggling when Jodie reached for the wax container and the Popsicle sticks. Jodie picked up a Popsicle stick and dipped it into the wax and spread a thick layer on Justin's chest. Justin bucked even more, because the wax was still pretty hot. Jodie then picked up a linen strip and placed it on Justin's bare chest. She pressed down and rubbed until the strip was stuck good. Without saying a word, Jodie grabbed one end of the linen strip and jerked it off in one quick motion. You could hear the wax-encrusted strip tear off the chest hair. The skin immediately turned red, and a few spots were beginning to bleed a little. As the strip was being ripped off, Justin made a muffled cry at the pain that ensued. Jodie enjoyed her actions more than she was willing to admit, but she wasn't finished yet. Justin had tears in his eyes by the time Jodie had finished his chest and worked down his stomach to his scrotum. There were small patches here and there of missing layers of skin, burn marks from the hot wax, and spots of blood from the improper application of the wax and the improper removing of the strips.

"Let's take a break, shall we?" Jodie stopped her victim's torture and picked up the wax container and made her way to the kitchen again to reheat the wax. Jodie returned from reheating the wax to see Justin lying still, as if his body had succumbed to death's cold embrace, but Jodie knew better. She knew how manipulative and tricky men could be, and she also knew as soon as she approached his bed and began with the waxing that he would have renewed strength to fight his bindings because her next area was his most treasured.

Jodie noticed she was almost out of linen strips and needed to make the most out of what was left. With an impish smile on her face, she intended to finish her work, and after placing the wax container on the nightstand, she reached into the box and picked up latex gloves and placed them on her hands, making sure to snap the wrist opening rather loudly. Justin jumped at the snaps and rolled his eyes in anguish at what was to come next. Jodie picked up a Popsicle stick and dipped one end into the hot wax. She extracted the wooden instrument and placed it directly on Justin's scrotum and spread out the material in a swirling pattern. Justin cried out a muffled cry at the scorching touch of the liquid wax. Jodie set the stick on top of the wax container's rim and picked up a linen strip and placed it on Justin and smoothed out the wrinkles and paused before she ripped it off of his skin. This part was the part Jodie had envisioned, the part that brought justice to fruition, and so far she wasn't disappointed. Gripping the edge of the strip, Jodie used one swift motion to remove it with a huge sigh while watching Justin's face turn red with rage and pain. His body began to buck wildly again. Jodie looked at her watch and decided that she had better make quick work of the last of her job, clean things up, and return home to wait for her life to unravel at the seams and Shayla's to begin to heal.

Justin bucked and jumped each time Jodie touched him, and when she had finished delivering all the retribution she had intended, she threw the used items away in the kitchen trash, picked up her box, and left Justin's house, leaving the front door unlocked. From beginning to end, Jodie's mission took her about an hour, and she was quite relieved when she arrived home and succumbed to her nightly ritual of a shower, a cup of hot tea, and a movie before retiring to her own bed. Shayla would be home tomorrow, and Jodie hoped, by some shred of a miracle, that Justin will have learned his lesson and would man up and move on.

*****

Three months worth of tomorrows came and went, and Jodie never saw hide nor hair of Justin. To her relief, the police never came calling. Some people who lived near Justin informed Jodie that within a week after Shayla's injuries, Justin put his house up for sale and moved out. The house has remained vacant ever since.

GABRIEL

Apprehension rose within me. I could feel my chest tightening, and my palms become clammy. Inside my head, I could hear the voices whispering to me again. I had learned long ago to shut them out most of the time, but at this moment it was almost impossible. There were too many.

I had stalked Gabriel for about six months now, waiting for the right time to turn him, and that time was now. As I stood outside a local nightclub waiting for him to come out, I wished I had brought a light sweater to protect me from the chill of the night air.

The voices were whispering more urgently now. "Take him … Take Him … *Take him now*!" they screamed inside my skull, so loud I thought it would split right open.

"Stop it! I know it's time," I said out loud to myself as I looked around and hoped no one on the street had heard me. There were few people out at this hour. It was about midnight, and most of the people were nestled in the safety of their homes, relaxing for the evening. But not me; I really wasn't one of them anymore.

The door opened from the nightclub with a loud bang as it hit the wall. Loud music poured out into the street as two people stumbled out. They were both giggling and falling all over each other. I tensed in anticipation, but noticed Gabriel wasn't one of them. I breathed a sigh of relief.

The voices were still going on in my head. They hovered in the background like a swarm of buzzing bees, but now was not the time to listen. I knew what I had to do, and at this moment I had to just wait.

I spied a shadow entering the open doorway, and out stepped a man. It was Gabriel. He stood nearly six feet tall. He was a large man, but not heavy. He was well built with light blond, wavy hair to his shoulders. He was, quite simply, handsome.

I felt a sick feeling in my stomach. As much as I felt compelled to do what the voices were saying, I was frozen in horror at the thought of taking Gabriel and turning him into a prince of the night. My veins may have cold blood running through them, but my heart isn't black. Not black like the Master. His heart was black and stone-cold, and he was ruthless and cruel. The elders were not much better. They always had their own agendas and would stop at nothing to see them fulfilled.

Gabriel stepped out into the night air as I made my way over to him.

"Hi, Sydney!" Gabriel called to me as he started to stroll in my direction.

"Hey!" I replied. My pale skin glistened in the moonlight, and my long chestnut hair flitted around my shoulders and across my face in the night's gentle breeze. Goose bumps made their way to the surface of my skin. I couldn't tell whether it was from the night air or from the mission that had to be completed this very evening. I remained frozen where I stood and allowed Gabriel to come to me.

"I missed you." Gabriel encircled his arms about my shoulders when he reached my side and gave me a good squeeze.

"I miss you back," I whispered in his ear as we walked toward my apartment.

The heart I did have was breaking at this very moment. I knew it was time, and he had no idea; this man, this human that I have fallen in love with. Of course, love between a daughter of the night and a human was forbidden, but our love would be allowed upon his rebirth.

Gabriel and I would never work out. I was a fool to think we could stay together forever without him turning. I knew as soon as I fulfilled my obligation to my clan that Gabriel would want nothing more to do with me. Every time in the past that I have turned someone, they have always felt betrayal and hatred toward me. I guess I can't blame them. I have taken their human existence away and thrown them into a world of darkness. But it was never for sport or for the joy of inflicting pain while draining them of their life fluids.

I warmed to Gabriel's touch. It was the only warmth I would ever feel. As I rested in his embrace, I noticed he smelled of cigarettes, beer, and aftershave. I can't stand the smell of cigarettes. I would have to make a note to try and get him in the shower as soon as possible.

We walked quietly and slowly. I could feel my Master's guardians around us. They were everywhere. They would make sure I fulfilled my job. If I didn't, then they would, and I could not bear for Gabriel to be touched by anyone else but me.

The breeze became stronger, and the night air had more of a chill.

"Sydney, why are you always so cold?" Gabriel asked me as he rubbed my bare arms.

I shrugged my shoulders and leaned my head against his chest. I would always feel cold. It would never change. I was forever trapped in a never-ending cycle of cold, loneliness, and pain.

We approached my apartment building and made the short climb up the few steps at the entrance. I unlocked the door, and Gabriel and I entered. We made our way down the darkened hallway to my apartment. The lights that lit the small hallway had been out for quite some time, and I had made several complaints to management about the situation, but to no avail.

As we entered my front door, Gabriel went to the kitchen, opened the refrigerator, pulled out a beer, made his way into the living room, and plopped down on my couch. He patted the cushion beside him for me to have a seat. I tossed my keys on an end table near the door and took my shoes off and tossed them to the side.

"Just a sec, OK?" I made my way around the room, lighting candles one by one and I closed the front window. The breeze had knocked over one of my potted plants on an end table, and I busied myself with cleaning up the small mess. I guess I would do anything to prolong the inevitable at this point.

It wasn't very long before the seductive scent of jasmine permeated the air, along with the soft amber glow of the candle flames. I glanced around my living room before my eyes settled on Gabriel.

The voices in my head had hushed, and it was easier to think. Should I just pounce on him and take him? Or should we make love and then, in the middle of it, take him? Either way he was bound to hate me and turn from me in disgust.

My heart was pained at the thought of taking away from Gabriel the very thing a human values most, his mortal life. If I did not, then I would be punished and driven from my clan. Not many vampires survive outside their clans. And that would be if I even survived the punishment. Rogue vampires were a thing of the past.

I have only heard about the punishment; I have never witnessed it. The Master, for some reason, favored me and shielded me from the horror. I believe it was my beauty that mesmerized him. It certainly wasn't my intellect. He had no use for that in a female. The Master believed the female was only good for following orders and jumping in the sack for a good time.

I put my cleaning rag in the kitchen sink and walked into the living room. I felt my pulse quicken as I sat down beside Gabriel. He slowly encircled his arms around me again and kissed my neck softly. It tickled my skin, as if a butterfly was gently beating its wings against me.

The vampire in me was making its way to the surface. I could feel my teeth elongate, and my mouth became dry. My heart beat rapidly, and the voices came to the forefront of my mind again. This time they weren't whispering. They were shouting, and I could not think, and I could not resist. It was my destiny. I had to fulfill my calling and help my clan survive.

Gabriel's turning would pave the way for my clan to enter the political arena in the human world. It really wasn't Gabriel they wanted, but his father's power and influence. The Master believed that if we turned Gabriel and made him one of us, it would give us some leverage with his father.

I pushed Gabriel off of me and positioned myself on his lap, facing him.

"Being a little aggressive tonight, are we?" Gabriel playfully teased.

I nodded my head in agreement and put my index finger to my lips in a hush sign. Gabriel grinned at me and rocked us off of the couch and onto the floor. We each made quick work of removing the other's clothing, and he took me there on the rug, and in the middle of our magic moment I went to bite him, but he had other plans.

In one swift motion, Gabriel reached under the sofa and pulled out a crudely made wooden stake. He pinned me to floor with one arm and raised the other with the stake and drove it home; straight through my heart. I felt an intense stabbing and burning sensation. Gabriel crawled off of my body, and I writhed back and forth across the rug a few times in agony.

"Did you really think I didn't know?" Gabriel said to me as my immortality came to end and my body turned to dust.

BIBLIOGRAPHY

"Aisling" is based on tales of Celtic Queen Boudicca/Boadicea from the Iceni tribe. I used the Web sites listed below for inspiration:

http://www.sheshen-eceni.co.uk/boudica_info.html
http://www.google.com
http://www.bbc.co.uk/history/historic_figures/boudicca.shtml

About the Author

Kimberly Bennett is a recently published independent author whose main goal is to provide readers of fiction a thrilling and memorable experience when they pick up one of her books and begin to read.

Kimberly has been a lifelong resident of Northeast Ohio and currently resides in Williamsfield. Kimberly attended and graduated from Kent State University where she earned a degree in Computer Technology.

Kimberly's debut short story collection, Twisted Delights, was originally released in October 2010. Since releasing Twisted Delights, Kimberly has been promoting her book at various conventions near Pittsburgh, PA.

CPSIA information can be obtained at www.ICGtesting.com
Printed in the USA
BVOW041331250112

281356BV00010B/10/P